D0055518

PIGEON PIE

NOVELS BY ROBERT CAMPBELL

ROBERT CAMPBELL

PIGEON PIE

THE MYSTERIOUS PRESS

Published by Warner Books

A Time Warner Company

Mysterious Press books are published by Warner Books, Inc.,
1271 Avenue of the Americas, New York, NY 10020.

 A Time Warner Company

The Mysterious Press name and logo are registered trademarks of Warner Books, Inc.

Printed in the United States of America

First printing: April 1998

10 9 8 7 6 5 4 3 2 1

Library of Congress Cataloging-in-Publication Data

Campbell, R. Wright.
    Pigeon pie / Robert Campbell.
      p.   cm.
    ISBN 0–89296–665–3
      1. Flannery, Jimmy (Fictitious character)—Fiction.
    2. Politicians—Illinois—Chicago—Fiction.   3. Chicago (Ill.)—
    Fiction.   1. Title.
    PS3553.A4867P5   1998
    813'.54—dc21   97-48921
                                                                        CIP

For Miranda

PIGEON PIE

One

Every once in a while I'm telling a story and somebody says, "You already told us that," so I stop right on the dime; I don't finish the story. Later on some other person who was in the group comes up to me and says, "Tell me the rest of that story you was telling the other night, Jimmy, I never heard it before."

Sometimes I ask the person how come they didn't speak up and they almost always say they didn't want to be the one to make the rest of the crowd listen to something they already heard. Like it's a great sacrifice to hear somebody's story more than once.

When somebody starts telling a story I heard before, I listen real close. You'd be surprised how much you can learn about a person by listening to how they tell a story more than once, even more than twice.

Also, I been told that every time I tell a story more than once I tell it without changing hardly a word except maybe here and there. I wonder what that says about me.

Anyway, I'm going to tell you a story I know you ain't heard before because this is the first time I'm telling it.

First, even though you might already know me, I'm going to tell you that my name's Jimmy Flannery and that, until recently, I'm the Democratic leader of the Twenty-seventh Ward in the great city of Chicago. Now I'm the committee-man in the Eleventh, which I won't say any more about because that's part of the story.

That's pretty much the way I introduce myself to new people that I meet, and I meet plenty.

"Hi, I'm Jimmy Flannery," I says. "I work for the Democratic Party in your ward. If there's anything I can do for you, let me know."

I been in precinct and ward politics ever since I went down to see Chips Delvin—God rest his soul—the warlord of the Twenty-seventh and the sewer boss of the city when I was only a kid of twenty, just a couple years out of high school. He gives me a job down in the pipes and tells me to go out and knock on doors for the party that election year.

I guess I did okay because by the time 1986 rolls around I'm an inspector, reading meters and doing paperwork, and I'm also a precinct captain in the Twenty-seventh.

That's also the year when I meet my wife, Mary Ellen Dunne, who's a nurse over to Passavant Hospital and a volunteer at an abortion clinic on Sperry which gets bombed.

The next year we get married and three years and some months after that we have a baby. We name her Kathleen. She's six years old now and I dearly love her.

Now there's another baby on the way.

Lately I find myself wondering, how did it happen? How did I get to be a married man with a kid and another on the way, the party leader of a city ward and a man who works behind a desk most of the time?

Mary's being thoughtful the other day, sitting in the chair by the front window, the lace curtain pushed aside, looking out on the street shining in the rain. I ask her what she's thinking and she says, "You ever think about chrysalides?"

"I beg your pardon?" I says.

"You know, chrysalises."

"You mean them hard cases caterpillars build around themselves so they can turn into butterflies?"

"That's right."

"Well, no, I don't think about them much," I says, humoring her a little bit—you know?—the way you should do with a pregnant woman.

"I wonder if the caterpillar, when it becomes a chrysalis, knows it's going to become a butterfly," Mary says.

"It's something to think about," I says.

"And do you think the butterfly, after it emerges from the chrysalis, remembers that it was once a caterpillar?"

"I'll give that a little thought, too," I says.

She smiles at me in a soft way like she understands I hardly know what she's talking about but she'll forgive me because only another woman could possibly understand what she's saying.

But I know what she's talking about. I think.

What's the difference between being asleep and dormant? Between being dormant and dead? Between being young and . . . before you know it . . . you're old?

If you know what being old is.

My old man always says, "Whenever a youngster gives me lip, I tell them the big difference between them and me is that I remember what it was to be their age but they don't know what it is to be my age."

Sometimes I feel like I'm getting old though I'm not yet even what they call, nowadays, middle-aged.

I didn't see the years go by. Like I was sleeping in a chrysalis. So, if up to now I been a caterpillar, does that mean when I come out of the chrysalis I'm in I'll be a butterfly?

Old friends like Mrs. Banjo and my old Chinaman Chips Delvin has passed away. And a lot of other people that I knew.

But I won't go into naming them all or even some of them. Enough to say that a good part of a ward committeeman's job is going to christenings, weddings and funerals. So I see a lot of beginnings, middles and endings.

My father, Mike, is still hale and hearty, married to Mary's mother, Charlotte, for some time now.

My dog, Alfie, is getting old, his muzzle so gray it looks like he's been dipping into a saucer of milk but he's still as eager for a walk as he was when he first come into my life.

Mary's Aunt Sada has something wrong with her hip but won't walk with a cane, stubborn as she is.

I see some little lines around Mary's eyes and mouth, but when I kiss them I don't know they're there and wouldn't care if I did.

I see some gray in my red hair. I rue the day when there'll be so much white in it that people'll start calling me "Pinkie."

After Delvin dies and leaves me the leadership of the Twenty-seventh Ward and his house in Bridgeport, a neighborhood what don't change very much, in the Eleventh Ward, I had to leave the six-flat . . . one of them converted into a mom-and-pop grocery store run by Joe Pakula and his sister, Pearl . . . in which I lived for years. I'd even bought a share in it to keep it from getting tore down.

We move into Delvin's house which is, luckily, almost as familiar to me as my own.

Mary laughs at me and says I'm turning into an old domesticated cat what don't like change. I'm still trying to figure out if that's a good thing or a bad thing. Me not wanting things to change I mean.

Last year I was offered a chance for a big change.

Leo the Lion Lundatos, the once powerful member of the United States Congress, indicted on thirty felony counts, which was mostly about fraud and abuse of privilege, ain't taking the loss of his seat in the last election without fighting back. He wants to establish a new power base by going back into city politics.

He wants to run for alderman of the Eleventh, known as the Mayor's Ward, and invites me to be his committeeman, otherwise known as the ward leader or warlord. It don't take a rocket scientist to see what he's up to. He has his eyes on being mayor one day even though he's seventy when he starts this new push for power. I got to hand it to him, the moxie he has.

I don't tell him that the alderman don't pick his own committeeman. It's an elective office decided during the regular party primaries. Although it's true that a deserving party worker can be appointed to the post by the state Democratic Party in the case of death or retirement, giving said deserving person a jump start when he or she comes up for election. But even though that happens to me when Delvin hands me the palm, it don't happen very often anymore.

Anyway, I don't correct him or remind him. I just mumble

something about me already being committeeman of the Twenty-seventh and very happy in my neighborhood.

I tell him I don't know why he wants me as the committeeman in the first place. If he wants to get back into politics by becoming the alderman in the Eleventh, there's plenty of people who'd be happy to oblige him.

I point out to him that I got a reputation for being something of a rebel and have refused more offers to join the club than you can count. He tells me that it's because I've got a reputation as an honest man, who honors his debts when he can and makes accommodations when he can't, that he wants me. He also adds that he'd been told I'm practically incorruptible, which I've learned is a remark in the same family as "trust me on this one."

Not that I want to sound cynical or ungrateful for the compliment. But I think that he's thinking an honest, incorruptible person makes a nice balance for hisself, who's carrying around the reputation of being something of a crook.

Of course, being a little bit of a crook is not altogether a bad reputation for a Chicago politician to have.

So I say thanks but no thanks.

But he persists, throwing a lot of tempting arguments in my face, not the least of which is his wife, Maggie. Not that she's ready to be bought or sold by Lundatos or anybody else, but there's an impression she gives that their marriage has sort of run out of steam and become just one of practical mutual benefit. There's a lot of power couples out there what stick together for the social and political convenience in being married. They got separate personal lives on the side but keep them under wraps.

It was whispered around that some of the "nieces" and "cousins" on his payroll when he was a congressman weren't there to take shorthand, especially one who was paid for working in Washington but lived in Chicago.

Even so he was pretty discreet compared to some.

Whether Maggie knew about the love nest Lundatos had set up in a building she owned before Fay Wray was found dead there, is a question to which I never did get a completely satisfying answer. And whether she had her own playmates and intimate companions unbeknownst to her husband or anybody else is another puzzler. There was no gossip going on about her at the time.

If she'd even consider such a thing, I'd bet a million any fooling around she might do would be with a person of her choice and not to satisfy any political aspiration Leo might have. Which don't mean that his accommodations and her accommodations couldn't coincide.

Whatever the situation, I still have the feeling when we meet that the offer's there if I want to reach out.

Anyway Lundatos's plan gets shot down when a new scandal breaks over his head. The call girl of mature age I just mentioned is found dead and his association with her is found out and there's about to be a cover-up. After we find out it's the call girl's husband what did her, Leo thinks he's going to walk off without a trace of mud on his cuffs.

I go to him with some tapes I obtain from Willy Dink, an old friend of mine who used to be an exterminator but is now into discreet investigations, and tell him that quitting the contest for alderman would be the smartest thing he could do.

He asks me if I'm one of those people who wouldn't mind if he got caught with his hand in the cookie jar but would mind very much if it got caught in a honey pot.

I tell him I ain't his conscience but that I do believe every candidate for public office should be better than he is at keeping his private affairs private.

He wants to debate the subject, trying to tie me up with considerations of special community standards, the greater good and other such diversions meant to twist the truth, but I don't go along with him. I tell him I'll do what I think I have to do if he goes ahead with building a new political career in the city. So he agrees never to run for public office again.

Which I don't entirely believe at that moment but which, the way things play out, could very well come true.

I think the indictments they got ready to bring against him will just blow away after he loses his congressional seat and drops out of the public eye. But the Republicans in Congress are on a roll and want to trash the Democrats every which way they can, so they let Lundatos know they ain't about to drop all of the charges against him. He's going to have to cut a deal and pay a price or go to trial.

Then these so-called informed rumors start sneaking out.

One of the defenses Lundatos supporters was using was the fact that under the rules then in place the Lion could've taken retirement and walked away with over a million dollars in unspent campaign contributions in his pocket. So what was all this nickel-and-dime stuff about crystal paperweights and a cousin on the payroll?

But his enemies start putting out the word that he has a stash of bribes and illegal contributions amounting to three times the million and he was staying in office as long as he could because he was hungry for more and wants to move the stash before some special prosecutor's men find it.

He cuts a deal and takes twenty-eight months in a Club Fed, one of them prisons without bars or fences set up for white-collar thieves, stock manipulators, extortionists, forgers and other such criminals against property instead of persons.

Fleece the innocent out of millions and have a vacation in a prison that could be a resort. Sell two ounces of pot and, in some states, pull ten hard.

It's another way the rich and well connected has of protecting themselves from the consequences of their crimes.

None of this spoils my chances for running for committeeman in the Eleventh if I decide to go ahead with it. In fact they get better.

The mayor calls me down to the fifth floor at City Hall and says, "I understand that our friend Leo Lundatos has decided to retire from public life."

"Yes, your honor, that's what I've been told," I says.

"Before he left on his retreat, he called to have a last chat, and told me he was ready to back you if you decided to run for alderman in the Eleventh."

"For committeeman, I think," I says.

"For alderman. For both if you want it. Even with Lundatos unable to run for office, Johnny O'Meara's getting tired of the game. He might be persuaded to step aside and grease the way for you. First he'll vacate the committeeman's job and sometime next year, before the elections, he'll retire from the city council, naming you his logical successor just before the voting."

"Why didn't O'Meara offer to retire so Lundatos could've been appointed to fill out his term?" I asks.

"Because Leo wanted to run and win just to prove the point to his enemies that he could make his comeback the hard way," the mayor says.

I'm thinking about what benefits O'Meara expected to get

from Lundatos even for not running for reelection, which after all would make the effort just that much easier.

What inducement will he expect from me for turning the jobs over to me without me even having to run for them the first time?

"You'll have six, seven months to make a mark on the council before you come up for election. That should give you a nice edge," the mayor says.

When I sit there without saying anything the mayor finally adds, "And you'll have my blessing, too."

I've got no reason *not* to believe his offer which, if you listen close enough, is not exactly an endorsement but more like a pat on the back for handling the business with Lundatos in a quiet and discreet manner.

However, though a blessing is nice it ain't exactly a promise of all-out support.

He's keeping his options open. You never know what tomorrow will bring.

Two

So I leave the mayor's office, ready to forget all about the offer or blessing or whatever you want to call it, but first I mention it to my old man just by way of handing him a laugh.

But he don't laugh. Instead, he's hardly able to contain the pride and pleasure he obviously feels having a son who shakes the hand of the mayor, who is the son of the mayor who once shook Mike's own hand. This mayor who, according to Mike, has definitely made me an offer to put a foot on the big ladder which becoming the committeeman and alderman in the Eleventh would be.

Some of you might wonder why being committeeman in the Eleventh should be more important than being the committeeman in the Twenty-seventh. Or why the alderman of one ward should have more clout than the alderman in another. Well, it's like they say, among equals there's always some people more equal than the others by reason of where they sit and who sat there before them.

"In a way the mayor was just keeping a promise he made to Lundatos," I says.

"How do you make that out?" Mike says.

"When the Greek wanted to rehabilitate hisself by entering local politics, first he convinced O'Meara it would be a good time to retire and let him slip in."

"With your help."

"For all he thought that was worth," I says.

"Which was plenty," Mike reminds me.

"Okay. So when Leo can't perform, the mayor's probably relieved at first. He don't need any critics accusing him of using his influence in behalf of a disgraced congressman under indictment. Then Lundatos makes a deal and takes the time. No chance of his running for anything. Which gives the mayor the opportunity to extend the favor he was going to extend to Lundatos to me."

"Yeah? So?"

"So it's an easy win for the mayor. He don't expect me to leave the Twenty-seventh. What reason would I have to do that without Lundatos pulling at me?"

"Yeah? So?"

"So it's like he's paying off his debt to Lundatos. Proving he's a man what keeps his word even when he's got no obligation to do so. Clearing his books."

"You got a very devious mind," Mike says, looking at me with what I can only call admiration. "But I see you got a genuine offer and I say you should take it."

I say I'll think about it, hoping that'll give Mike enough time to forget about it, but I don't intend to think about it and he don't intend to forget about it.

He practically gets on the six o'clock news, broadcasting

the word of the mayor's offer to everybody he meets. Naturally he tells the family and they all get as excited as him.

Charlotte and Sada are all for it. Charlotte because she sees a better life for her daughter and grandchildren, Sada because she thinks I'm the most honest politician, next to her dead husband, Monroe Spissleman (Mo Spice, the Socialist), she's ever known.

Wally Dunleavy, who sits there in his office running Streets and Sanitation, hearing every fly that farts in the entire city, the oldest and trickiest civil servant I know, calls me the next morning and tells me to grab the offer while the grabbing's good.

Janet Canarias, the lipstick lesbian alderwoman of the Twenty-seventh, says how proud she'd be to sit on the council with me and help bring some justice into the system.

After a show of reluctance, Mary admits that she wouldn't mind if I went for it. Why not? Why shouldn't a man's wife want to see her husband rise in the world? But she makes it clear she's not going to say any more about it. It's got to be what I want and she won't try to influence me.

Well, I could go on, but for them what knows me and also knows the friends I'm happy to have, I'll just leave the subject by mentioning the fact that everybody I ever knew says I should run.

Even Lundatos calls me from the federal prison camp in Duluth and tells me to go for it.

"Jimmy," he says, "this is the Lion."

"Hello, Mr. Lundatos," I says. "What can I do for you?"

"Call me Leo, Jimmy. Will you do that? Whatever happened I still think of you as a friend and I hope you feel the same about me."

"I got no reason to think otherwise, Leo," I says.

"Well, I'm certainly glad to hear that. You know, Jimmy, when we met at old Chips Delvin's funeral I took to you right away. I admit I wanted your help but that don't change the fact that I liked you right off the bat."

I don't know what else to say so I say, "Thank you, Leo."

"We both lost a good friend and mentor in old Delvin. So, what I'm gong to suggest here may seem a presumption but I'm going to say it anyway."

When he pauses, I says, "What's that?"

It's a politician's trick he pulled on me. He gets me to ask a question to show I'm interested so he can make it look like I'm the one instigated the conversation, otherwise he never would've brought it up.

"I'm older than you, just like Delvin was older than me, so maybe I know a couple things could be useful to you just like Delvin taught me a couple tricks. I never stopped keeping my eye on Chicago all them years I was in Washington, so I ain't completely uninformed about the ins and outs of city politics."

"Nobody could accuse you of not knowing the ins and outs," I says, which I immediately see could be taken as a comment about some of what got him here in prison.

He sees it too. "Is that a little joke, there, Jimmy?"

"I didn't mean it that way. I just meant—"

"Let it go. Let it go. I guess I'm just getting sensitive, being up here and all. Anyway, what I want to say is that I'm ready to give you what advice and counsel I can, just like our grand friend Delvin used to do."

"I appreciate the offer, Leo. If anything comes up, I'll certainly get in touch."

"I'm talking specifically about you taking over as committeeman in the Eleventh. And about you maybe running for the aldermanic seat. I think I can help you with your strategy there. I'd like to do that for you. Will you do that for me?"

"Do what?"

"Let me help you?"

"I'll certainly do that," I says.

"You want to get in touch call me at this number anytime," he says. Then he gives me the number. Then he says, "If I'm not available you can leave a message on my voice mail."

"You got voice mail?"

"Well, I got to keep up with my affairs, Jimmy. I ain't going to be here forever."

After we hang up I sit there thinking about what it is Lundatos wants or will want from me. The way it works is you get somebody in your debt for doing them favors you maybe even forced on them so that, later on, you can ask the other person to balance the books and do you a favor.

A couple of days after that—I don't know if Leo puts her up to it—Maggie Lundatos sends me word that there's no hard feelings over how I handled the thing with her husband and would I like to sit down with her and have a chat.

I think about that one a long time, but finally I send her a note, thanking her for her generosity and interest, but saying I don't know when I can find the time to have a meeting with her.

I'm very pleased with myself, thinking what a mature and prudent thing it is for me to do. Avoiding Maggie Lundatos like that. This older woman who, since I met my wife, is the only woman who ever stirs certain strong feelings in me.

Three

For almost a week, I don't tell anyone about this request from Maggie Lundatos. I tell them about the call I get from Lundatos but I don't mention the note I get from Maggie.

If I ain't going to make any career moves, if I'm going to stay right where I am as warlord of the Twenty-seventh, helping Janet Canarias, who's the alderman, and helping the people in my neighborhood, who I know all my life, then I don't see any reason to mention Maggie. Especially since I doubt I'll ever see her again except maybe we bump into one another at some political function or party fund-raiser.

On the other hand, if you can learn anything from some of the shenanigans that have been going on the last several years in Washington, D.C., it's that the crimes and misdemeanors ain't what causes most of the trouble the politicians get themselves into. It's the cover-ups. You got nothing to hide, why hide it?

On the other hand, there's the one about letting sleeping dogs lie.

On the other hand . . .

On Saturday afternoon—it's the first week in April and I pretend that I can smell spring—I go take a walk with Alfie, who's a lot slower on his feet than he used to be. Which I suppose you could also say about me. I like talking things out with Alfie because he'll look at me from time to time as though having a conversation but he'll never make any comments except for an occasional sigh. Also I know he ain't going to lay down any judgments on things I might admit—like lusting in my heart after beautiful and desirable women, the way our ex-president Jimmy Carter once confessed he sometimes did, much to his regret—and he sure ain't going to go around blabbing any confidences to anybody.

"I been married . . . what? . . . ten years now?" I says.

Alfie gives me a sidewise and upward look as though to say, "Work it out, fella. If you been married ten years that also means Mary's been married ten years."

"I ain't saying I never looked at a nice pair of legs or balconies but that's all I ever done, just looked," I says. "But this Maggie . . . I don't know what it is about her . . . could maybe light a fire I don't want lit. You see what I'm saying?"

Alfie blinks at me as though he sees very well what's going on here.

"What I'm thinking is I could avoid altogether meeting with Maggie Lundatos, even though it means giving up any influence she could have with people who might throw some votes my way. Just in case I should decide that it might not be a bad idea for me to run for alderman in the Eleventh, you understand?"

He blinks. Of course he understands, his look says. I've been gotten to. All the flattery's gone to my head. I'm walking around protesting that I don't want to put my foot on the fast track but here I am tying the laces on my running shoes.

"I'm doing the smart thing," I says. "I'm avoiding temptation."

Alfie coughs, like it's all he can do not to call me a liar.

"Of course, there's common courtesy," I says. Then very quickly I add, "Which is not to say I feel obligated to meet with her. I'm just wondering if we ain't got a case of me presuming too much. I mean whatever I felt them two times we met, under entirely different circumstances, could've been a passing emotion."

Alfie glances up. He's saying that, yeah, the circumstances are different. Now there ain't going to be any husband standing by.

"Sure, it could be just a case of common courtesy. An acquaintance wants to meet with me, why shouldn't I meet with her? Maybe she needs a favor. I do favors for people every day. Why shouldn't I do her a favor? On the other hand, I'm sure she's got plenty of people ready to do her a favor."

Alfie tosses me another look as though to say there's nothing he likes better than a man who can make up his mind.

"So the only question is, should I tell Mary about Maggie's invitation to have a chat?"

Alfie don't say yes, he don't say no, but I get the feeling he's saying that if you're worried about whether you should tell your partner something, then you probably should tell your partner something. But be careful what you say. It's not a good idea to go in for what-ifs, the bare bones should suffice. On the other hand it's never a good idea to withhold anything and certainly not to downright lie.

I point out to Alfie that men have been lying to their wives by not telling the whole, unvarnished truth since the world began.

And look at the trouble that's caused, Alfie says with his look.

"Why poke the cat when it's smiling in its sleep?" I says.

Alfie lifts his leg against a tree. I take it as his final comment.

So I go back to the house and ask Mary is it all right we ask my father and her mother, Aunt Sada and Janet Canarias over for supper the next night.

Also I invite Willy Dink, who used to be an environmentally correct vermin exterminator, living in a wood butcher's van with a dog, a ferret, a snake and other assorted natural enemies of roaches, spiders, ants, mice and rats, who then becomes a private investigator of sorts. More like a surveillance expert since he's learned how to crawl into the smallest spaces and plant listening and spying devices in unlikely places.

I think I already told you that he was the one got me the tapes on Leo Lundatos visiting the love nest which Lundatos claimed he knew nothing about.

He's living in our old apartment over on Polk Street now after I got the rest of the people in the building to let him keep his animals of which he's still got a few.

After a meal of chicken, green beans, mashed potatoes and Irish soda bread, I help Mary stack the dishes in the new dishwasher while the others have coffee and dessert in the living room.

Then I join them with my own cup. Mary brings a glass of water with her, having given up coffee altogether since she learned about the new pregnancy.

"This is all quite grand," Mike says, "coffee and dessert in the living room."

"I was just thinking the same thing," Charlotte says.

"We never had the room before," Mary says.

"A suitable setting for an alderman," Sada says.

"Well, I don't know," I says. "I wouldn't go up against Janet here. I'll just hang on as committeeman in our ward and help her out every way I can."

"I was thinking alderman of the Eleventh," Sada says.

"I thought we agreed to shelve that for a while," I says.

"Jim Buckey, the new chairman of the Democratic Party, thinks it's an option," my father says.

"Johnny O'Meara's ready to step down if you'll take the offer," Janet Canarias says. "You could fill out his term by appointment and be settled in long before you had to campaign for the job."

"He'll step aside as committeeman, maybe," I says.

"Step aside for both committeeman and alderman is the suggestion he made to me when I spoke to him at City Hall day before yesterday."

"Didn't the mayor, hisself, practically say as much?" my father says.

"You should know better'n me that practically don't count for much," I says. "I ain't had any conversations with Johnny O'Meara lately."

"Then maybe it's about time you did," Sada says.

"You could pick up both jobs," my father says, like he didn't even hear my doubts and objections. "You could be the power in the Eleventh and then who knows what?"

"Why are we telling James all this?" Charlotte asks in her soft voice. "He knows it all just as well as we do and I'm sure he's thought about it a lot more than we have."

I understand that Charlotte's trying to be like a mother to me even though I was far too old for any of that sort of thing when she met and married my father after I was already married to her daughter. But I can tell she's getting as conflicted as I am about this whole business and is ready to come down on my side whatever I decide to do.

Then Mary, who wasn't going to speak about it again, finally drops in a word.

"What's the real reason for this family conference, James?" she asks.

And right there I know I've made up my mind to go for it and Mary knows it too. And knows that there's something else besides their blessing I want them to give me their judgment on.

"Leo and Maggie Lundatos," I says, feeling the relief of getting the cat out of the bag.

"What about them?" Mary says.

"Leo's in Club Fed cooking up gourmet Greek meals for the other three or four inmates in his cottage," Mike says. "Maybe working on his waistline pumping a little iron, working in the garden. Maybe just sunning hisself."

"He called me and offered his advice and support."

"Is it Maggie you're wondering about?" Sada asks, giving me the shrewd eye. "You afraid she'll muster the considerable influence she's got against you because you were the one helped put her husband out of business?"

"What're you talking about, Sada?" Mike says. "The word's going around that Maggie Lundatos is ready to leave a sinking ship."

"That doesn't necessarily mean she's developed a liking for Jimmy."

"The fact is," I says, "she sent me a message telling me she forgives me for anything I did concerning Leo."

Mike doesn't get it but the women get it. Especially Mary.

"When did Maggie Lundatos get in touch with you, James?"

"Oh, maybe a week. Almost a week."

"And all she wanted to do was forgive you?"

"She wants to sit down and have a chat."

"Very nice. Very nice," my father says. "She's got friends. A few of those upmarket cocktail parties and afternoon teas, and you can sleep through the elections when the time comes."

"That's a long way to go," I says.

"No reason in the world you can't start building your organization and lining up your support, sooner instead of later," Sada says.

All of a sudden the conference turns into a victory celebration for something that could never happen, everybody except Mary and me acting like it's a done deal.

I know she's still thinking about Maggie Lundatos who, if the rumors is true, may soon be a gay divorcée.

There's no way of stopping it. The good feelings and

confident chatter go on for another hour and then everybody goes home.

Willy Dink's the last to leave, having sat through dinner
and the conversation in the living room afterward without
saying hardly a word.

"I want to thank you for including me in your family
conference," he says.

"I value your opinion, Willy," I says.

"So you won't mind if I give you a little piece of advice?"
he says.

"That's what I'm asking for," I says.

"Stay away from that white-haired woman," he says.
"She's a charmer but she can bring you harm."

Then he ducks his head and slips away down the stairs
and into the shadows like he does.

Mary and me look in on Kathleen, who's sleeping like an
angel, and then we get ready for bed.

Once under the covers, laying there looking up at the
shadows of the trees on the ceiling, Mary says, "What are
you afraid of, sweetheart?"

While I'm thinking about how I'll answer the question,
she goes on. "Have you got feelings for Maggie Lundatos?"

"I don't know if it's what you'd call feelings."

"A fascination?"

"An interest in what makes her tick," I says, tiptoeing all
around the question. "I'd never do anything about it, whatever it is." Right away I know that's exactly the wrong thing
to say.

"I know you wouldn't," Mary says. "Not if you could
help yourself."

I start to say I wouldn't, nohow, no way, but Mary cuts

me off. "I'm going to be getting big and unattractive pretty soon and, if you accept her help, you'll be with that beautiful, powerful woman as much as you'll be with me and—"

I roll on my side and put my hand on Mary's belly.

"Hey," I says, "you could never be less than the most beautiful woman in the world to me."

She smiles and kisses me before I can say anything more. "We'll just leave it at that for now, will we, Jimmy? You go have a meeting with Maggie Lundatos. You go get a seat on the city council."

Four

It's getting so that when it ain't an election year it's a campaign year at practically every level of elective office from the president of the United States down to the guy running for sheriff in some county in the remotest corner of the country.

When they're not actually campaigning, the average politician is out there fund-raising, because it's getting so you got to mortgage the kids and hock the wife in order to stay in the game. It's worse than cutthroat poker.

But, officially, the state of Illinois runs five elections, two in even-numbered and three in odd-numbered years.

Except for Chicago. Since Chicago don't elect township or special district officials, and city officials serve for four years, the city only has two and two.

Which means that in even-numbered years there's a general primary election the third Tuesday in March which includes a presidential preference, party nominations for election the following November and the election of various political party officers like the delegates and alternatives to the national convention, state central committeemen and Chicago ward committeemen.

In November we vote for the electors for president and vice president, U.S. senators, one every six years from 1986 and one every six years from 1990, a representative to Congress from each district, state officers like the governor, lieutenant governor, secretary of state, and so forth.

Plus state senators, representatives and trustees of the University of Illinois.

Also the Cook County Board president, commissioners, clerk, sheriff, treasurer, assessor, board of appeals, superintendent of educational service region, state's attorney, recorder of deeds, and circuit court clerk, judges of the supreme, circuit and appellate courts, and three members of the Metropolitan Sanitary District.

I could be missing somebody here but I don't think it matters very much.

Which brings us to the odd-numbered years.

In February there's a consolidated primary on the last Tuesday of the month for which Chicago voters declare their party affiliation so they can vote for party nominations for the April elections. But they don't have to declare to vote for aldermen, which is not a primary but a final. Unless no candidate in the ward receives a majority of votes cast, in which case a runoff in the April election decides the winner.

The April election selects the mayor, city clerk, city treasurers and any runoff aldermen, plus library district officers and a few other elected public servants.

Now you know as much about Chicago elections as ninety percent of the politicians in office.

One more thing could be of interest. The consolidated election takes place every four years after 1987.

Candidates for alderman file with the Chicago Board of Elections seventy-one to seventy-eight days before the election, which is a big problem for a lot of candidates, but not for me. If O'Meara keeps his promise I'll be getting a handout like some people say I've always got.

First Delvin giving me a job with the city when I was just a couple of years out of high school. Then him giving me the job of precinct captain. Later on, after I put in my time and he's growing old, he hands me the job of ward committeeman on a silver platter.

Don't get me wrong here, it wasn't exactly a gift. Some people might think that walking the sewers all them years was walking through whipped cream but I'm here to tell you it ain't. Neither is it easy on the feet to go around the neighborhood knocking on doors, asking if there's anything anybody needs doing that, maybe, I can help with.

And being the ward leader, listening to everybody's troubles, is guaranteed to keep you jumping.

So now I'm ready to pick up both jobs, committeeman and alderman in the Eleventh, if things go the way they're supposed to go, without getting a signature on a petition or even knocking on a door.

Which is not to say it's going to be a free ride altogether. I'm going to have to build an organization and run for committeeman and alderman sooner or later.

I'm walking along thinking about all this when I wake up to the fact that I'm on Polk Street in the old neighborhood. There's the old six-flat with the corner one converted into a mom-and-pop grocery store. It feels like I been away for twenty years though it's been, maybe, twenty months.

I ain't stopped by Joe and Pearl Pakula, what own the corner grocery, or dropped in on the Recores what used to live across the hall from me, in all that time, though I get the word about them, here and there.

Two of their kids are dead, one shot in a mugging and the other of some sickness, and the rest are all scattered.

And I ain't seen Myron and Shirley, who live on the second floor with their little girl who ain't a little girl anymore. Or John Henson, the black cop, and his family who're living where Mrs. Foran and Miss King used to live.

There's a For Sale sign on the door to the vestibule.

Everybody was talking about putting it up for sale about the time Mary, Kathleen and me moved, and I signed a paper saying I agreed to listing the building with a real estate agent. Did I think it was never going to happen? Did I think it was always going to be there, unchanged, so I could go back anytime I got lonely for the past and there it'd be, waiting for me?

I go into the grocery store looking for Joe and Pearl but they ain't there.

There's a young black man behind the counter.

"You working for Pearl and Joe?" I asks.

"I'm not working for anybody but myself," he says, showing me a little bit of attitude.

"Hold it. That was a question not an observation. I used to live in this building—"

"I'm the new owner of this building," he says. "Which tenant was you?"

I stick out my hand. "I'm Jimmy Flannery. I'm the Democratic ward leader in the Twenty-seventh."

"Oh, yeah," he says, taking my hand and losing the attitude. "I heard lots about you."

"All bad I expect," I says, working the old joke.

"Some good, some bad," he says, and gives me a white smile could blind a person.

"I didn't know the old building was sold," I says.

"We're just clearing escrow. That's why the sign's still up. I'm hoping you'll see my name on the transfer papers in a couple weeks, the latest."

"Your name, you say?"

"Ron Jordan," he says.

"Is everybody who owned a flat out of there?" I asks.

"The Jewish couple and their daughter's gone. Also the Recores on the top floor."

"Yeah, across from me."

"Willy Dink's?"

"How's that working out?"

"We got no mice, ants or cockroaches in the building," he says, grinning.

"How about the Hensons?"

"They're staying."

"Mrs. Bilina?"

"Gone."

"Joe and Pearl?"

"Gone. All gone," Jordan says.

I stand there, a man without a reason for being there. I know that Jordan's watching me.

"Hey, what's the problem?" he says. "I heard you went on to bigger and better."

"Well, I went on to bigger," I says.

Five

O'Meara sends word he'd like to see me over to Schaller's Pump.

When I walk through the door, it's like every white-haired Irish political type in the city has stopped in for a bite and a beer. There's a lot of white-haired Italians and Polish, too, but it's the Irish way of not looking at you straight on but seeing everything about you that tells me they're mostly Irish.

But Irish or whatever, when I walk in the door all these sidelong glances tells me I've been the subject of the conversations at practically each and every table.

That and the fact that Johnny O'Meara's sitting at a table all alone, waving and grinning at me, everybody giving us what passes for privacy in the Pump.

"What's your pleasure, Jim?" O'Meara asks, shaking my hand.

"A glass of ginger ale."

He gets up and goes over to the bar to order it hisself.

When he comes back he sets it down in front of me, then sets hisself down and folds his hands on his vest.

"What can I do for you?" he asks.

"I decided to take you up on your offer," I says.

"What offer's that?"

"To step down as committeeman in the Twenty-seventh and let the chairman of the Democratic Committee—"

"Jim Buckey," he says, interrupting me like I don't know that Buckey's the new party leader.

"—appoint me to finish out your term of office," I says, giving him the nod to thank him for reminding me who's chairman. "Then, later on, to do the same for the aldermanic seat."

"I don't remember making such an offer," O'Meara says, giving me the whole sleepy-eye, droopy-lid look of a man about to cut a deal.

"It's possible I misheard you but the mayor, hisself, mentioned it last time I seen him. So you can understand my confusion," I says.

"What I probably said was that I wouldn't run against Lundatos and if he wanted you as his committeeman, I wouldn't run against you either. In the next elections that is. When that time comes."

"Hold on a second here," I says. "You know a fellow by the name of Jake O'Meara?"

"Sure, I know Jake. He was a cop, once upon a time."

"He a relative?"

"No, he's no relative. He ain't even a friend. I just know him. What's this Jake O'Meara got to do with this discussion?"

"You know how in a book, there's never two characters

with the same name? I don't understand that. I mean I got at least five friends named O'Meara."

"It's a pretty common name," he says, frowning now. "Person writes a book he don't want to use the same name for two characters. It'd make for considerable confusion."

"That's what I'm thinking right now. I'm really not sure which O'Meara I'm talking to. Because the Johnny O'Meara who makes this offer to me, after Leo Lundatos decides to leave politics, is the warlord of this ward and a man known for his golden promises."

"Still is and always will be," O'Meara says. "Why you hitting such a long ball?"

"Because it's very hard for me to come right out and call you a welcher. Because I'm hoping you'll jump in here and tell me that you're just pulling my leg a little bit and not waiting for me to make an offer."

"Can we review what you say I said or think I said?" he asks.

"The mayor, hisself, told me that I'd have your blessing if I decided to run for alderman in the Eleventh."

"For committeeman, Jimmy. For committeeman."

"Not for alderman? No blessing for that?"

"I always wish anyone well who decides to run for public office in my ward," he says.

"But not anyone who wants your council chair?"

"Well, a man's chair is his comfort, Jimmy. Don't you know?"

"I think maybe I got to get my hearing checked."

"It don't hurt to have a complete physical once a year, Jimmy," he says.

Then he says, "The basic offer I'm making you is for me

not to run against you for committeeman in the next election."

"Thank you for the generous offer, Johnny, but that ain't what I had in mind. I'll just stay in the Twenty-seventh where I don't have to take any favors to keep the job."

"Well, think of it this way, Jimmy. You come over and be my committeeman and the chances of me giving up the council seat sometime soon, considering my age and all, is a lot better than the chances of Janet Canarias giving up hers. And I don't think you could take it away from her."

"I wouldn't try. She's a friend," I says, putting my hands on the table like I'm ready to get up and leave.

"Wait a second. Wait a second," O'Meara says, looking at the clock above the bar. "Finish your ginger ale."

"I already had enough," I says.

The phone rings behind the bar. O'Meara whips his head around, like it's something he expected. The bartender reaches the phone, which is on a long cord, over the wood.

"This is John O'Meara," O'Meara says, waving me to sit down, me standing there stooped over, half in, half out of the chair.

He listens for maybe thirty seconds. "Yes, he's here." He hands the handset to me.

"This is Jimmy Flannery," I says.

"Hello, James," Maggie Lundatos says. "I understand you're having a glass of ginger ale with my good friend John O'Meara."

"Well, he's having a beer," I says.

"Always a stickler for the facts, aren't you, James?"

"Not always."

"But you recognize a fact when you see one?"

"A piano don't have to fall on me before I hear the tune," I says.

"Did you not get my message?"

"I sent you a note explaining how with the new house and all—"

"I understand," she says, cutting me off. "You're a very busy man. Some of us have so much time on their hands that we're looking for things to do."

"Like a hobby?"

"No, like a serious enterprise or endeavor. Have you given my offer of support any more thought?"

"That's why I've been so long getting back to you," I says.

"So what have you decided?"

"I've decided to accept it," I says, staring at O'Meara so there's no doubt he hears the message.

"I'm very happy to hear that," she says. "We must have a chat."

"You want to make an appointment now?" I asks.

"Why don't you call me in a day or two, Jimmy, and we'll set it up," she says.

So it ain't James anymore. She's just moved the relationship up a notch.

She hangs up. I hand the telephone to O'Meara.

"On second thought," he says, "not only will I step aside and let Buckey appoint you committeeman of the Eleventh but I can tell you right now that, when the time comes, I won't be running for another term as alderman."

That's the way it's done, Chicago style.

O'Meara's sitting there waltzing around with me waiting for me to make an offer, sweeten his drink some way, if not in cash then in kind. Favor for favor. Big favor for big favor.

Only he's already got a negotiation going with Maggie

Lundatos and he's waiting for her call while we do the old two-step.

When the call comes he knows that Maggie's accepted a deal they already discussed, a little something for his retirement, a guaranteed place at the table in his old age. Whatever.

I'm beginning to realize that, disgraced husband or no disgraced husband, Margaret Lundatos is an even bigger player than I ever thought she was.

That evening I'm sitting on my front porch with my old man, the way people used to do before television drove them all indoors.

"You made up your mind?" he says.

"I went down to see Johnny O'Meara at Schaller's Pump this afternoon."

"Is he ready to step aside the way he told you he would?"

"I got taught a little lesson first."

"How's that?"

"It was made very clear that I couldn't run alone. That I could use a little help."

"You already knew that. Nothing new in that."

"Janet ran against the tide and won."

"Different times. Reform was in the air. New constituencies forming. But things are settled down again. You got to stay on the path if you want to get anywhere, nowadays. They say the party system's almost dead and the machine busted. Well, the principles are just the same. The basics don't change."

"I'm not complaining. I'm just not sure I can play in this league."

"Which league is this you're talking about?"

I tell him about the horsing around O'Meara and me go through in more detail. How Maggie Lundatos puts in the call cutting a deal with O'Meara so he'll cut the deal with me.

"You feel like you been fooled into accepting her support?" Mike asks.

"I ain't sure how I feel."

"You think, if you turned her down, O'Meara would've stayed where he is?"

"He could've thrown his support, and the party's support, to somebody more acceptable to Maggie Lundatos."

"If good people don't want to play because the game's too rough, we're in one hellofalot of trouble, Jimmy."

"You staying for supper?" I asks.

"No, Charlotte's waiting for me. I just stopped by to see Kathleen when she came home from school. She's getting so big."

"You feeling all right, Pop?"

"Oh, sure," he says, starting to get up out of the wicker rocking chair. But it's an effort and I have to stand up and steady him with a hand under his arm. He looks at me with eyes so sad it almost breaks my heart.

"Old bones," he says. "Old bones."

He stands there at the top of the steps.

"Another spring," he says.

Then he looks at me with them blue eyes he's got which seem to get paler and paler every year.

"Is it just you're annoyed you was traded like a bonus player?" he asks. "Or is it being closer to Maggie Lundatos that's got you worried?"

"It's something to worry about, ain't it?"

He shakes his head. He's had his adventures with ladies

other than his wives. I don't know if it ever bothered his conscience much or any.

Then he says, like he's reading my thoughts, "Let your conscience be your guide."

Six

The first time I had occasion to meet Maggie Lundatos was over to the Last Chance Saloon, which is not to be confused with Dan Blatna's Sold Out Saloon where me and my old man used to have kielbasa and cabbage every Wednesday night. We practically never get together like that anymore what with me being married with a kid and another on the way, and him being married to Mary's mother.

The first time I told you about Maggie, I said she was a handsome woman maybe fifty-nine or even sixty, but I since find out she's really fifty-six, having been married to Burke, her first husband, when she was only sixteen and Lundatos when she was eighteen.

Anyway, whatever her age, she's one of them women spreads this cool sexual appeal around, giving you ideas without really making it too obvious to anybody else.

The next time I see her back then is at Cricket's, this up-market little restaurant in the Tremont Hotel, where a lot of the city's movers and shakers, especially the ladies, like to gather for lunch.

This time I see that she ain't just handsome, she's drop-dead beautiful. The white hair, the blue eyes and the milky skin with a faint spray of freckles across her nose and a subtle slash of pink on her mouth make a picture it's very hard to resist.

The only other time we ever even speak is once on the telephone when it was announced in the newspapers that Leo was making a deal and would serve some time. But we ain't talked or bumped into one another since.

Her message, what comes to my office machine the next morning, reminding me about making an appointment like I agreed to do over at the Pump, is a nice and very subtle gesture. I was supposed to call her to ask for a meeting, which is supposed to put me in the psychological position of being the one who asked. Now what's she done is make herself the one who's asking. Letting me be alpha pup, if you know what I mean, although she suggests a time and place which, if you think about it, still makes her the one calling the tune.

When I call her, I get her machine. I leave a message confirming the time and place.

That evening I stop by the office and there's a message from her confirming my confirmation.

I notice lately that more and more of everyday business is conducted on machines. Mary even talked me into getting a computer. Kathleen's learning how to use one in school. For God's sake the baby's only six and already she's talking to me about megahertz and gigabytes and whatever.

Which might be okay but, when it comes to talking, a face-to-face is always best. Failing that, an actual person on the other end of the phone line is better than a machine message any day of the week.

So now I'm walking into the rich gloom of Cricket's to meet with Maggie Lundatos again. It comes to me with something like a shock that this is only the third time I'll be seeing her but I got the feeling that I'm about to see an old sweetheart I ain't seen for years.

I'm standing at the entrance, looking around, when Maggie stands up like she's spotting herself for me. She's wearing a dress in a color of blue that matches her eyes exactly. It's got a very short skirt and a wide pink belt that cinches in her waist. It looks to me like she's lost a couple of pounds but that could be the new hairdo which ain't the way it was, sort of flying all over the place, but shorter, more like the way Myrna Loy wore her hair in those Thin Man movies.

"Jimmy," she calls. "Jimmy, over here." Every woman in the place looks at me and knows that Maggie's laid a claim on me.

Then she sits down.

While I'm crossing the room, a waiter's crossing from the other direction, so that when I sit down he's putting a glass of ginger ale with a maraschino cherry in it on the table in front of me.

"Ginger ale, isn't that your drink?" Maggie asks.

"Sometimes I have a Diet Coke or an iced tea," I says.

"If you'd rather have something else . . ."

"No, no. I was just teasing you a little bit."

"For presuming?" she asks.

I give a little shrug and she smiles.

"I promise not to presume too much," she says, reaching over to take the cherry from my ginger ale.

"You're not offended, me teasing you?" I asks.

"Teasing is good, Jim. Teasing can be very good. You'll be happy to know I didn't order your lunch. Are you still watching your weight?"

"I'm doing what I can."

The waiter's back waiting for our orders.

"The usual for me, Fred," she says, and raises her eyebrow to let me know it's my turn.

"I'll have the same," I says, letting her know I trust her good taste. Also that I'm a man that ain't afraid of taking a chance and breaking his own rules now and then. A second later I'm worrying if she'll take it as flirtation.

"Are we through with the foreplay?" she asks.

I get the feeling that there's going to be a lot of these double entendres flying around. Or maybe it's just like there's a million ordinary things a person can say that mean nothing in one context and all sorts of things in another. If she's worried about presuming too much, I better be just as careful about doing the same.

"I guess we know each other well enough to speak right out without pussyfooting around," I says.

"But that's just it, Jim, we hardly know each other at all. We've only met three times and—"

"Twice," I says, putting a word in there.

"—and spoken on the telephone a few more."

"Once," I says.

She smiles a little and I know I put my foot in a trap. Now she knows I been thinking about her because I remembered details men usually don't remember about a woman.

"We're not much more than the most casual of acquaintances yet you've affected my life more than practically any other man I've ever known," she goes on. "Except for my father, my Uncle Joe and my husbands."

I let the remark lay there. It ain't the kind of remark I want to pick up.

But she won't let it lay there.

"Would you like to know in what way you've affected my life?"

I still don't say anything, but I got to do something, so I nod.

"Well, my father, Joseph Cooley, gave me life, so his importance is obvious. My Uncle Joe introduced me to Charlie Burke, and the divorce settlement two years later laid the foundation of my fortune. Leo's influence is obvious. He was my lover, my husband, my friend and my teacher. He taught me the ways of the world. Whatever sophistication I've got came from the opportunities to move among the powerful which he gave me. I already knew how to move among the rich."

"Don't it take one to be the other?" I says.

"You're not rich, Jim, but you're a powerful man."

I shake my head, more than a little bit embarrassed at the intensity of the way she's looking at me.

"You are, even if you don't know it yet. There are men marked out for a special fate. You can rise a long, long way if you want to."

Now that I've been buttered, I wonder is it finally time for her to stick a fork in me?

"I'd like to help you get wherever that may be," she says.

"I thank you for your interest," I says.

"That's very polite," she says, almost snapping at me. "I'm not offering to make a cash contribution to one of your pet charities. I'm ready to put a significant fraction of my assets on the line to see you run a winning campaign for any political position you care to go after. I'm willing to throw all of my political influence, which is not insignificant, into the pot as well.

"You've got a little look on your face," she goes on. "If I wanted to be unkind, I could even call it a smirk. You're probably thinking that a man like yourself, who's spent his whole life in neighborhood politics, doesn't need the help and advice of the wife of a disgraced, imprisoned congressman."

"I wasn't thinking—" I start to say, but she cuts me off like she's cutting my throat.

"I said the foreplay was over," she says in a low voice. "It's time to fuck or forget it."

That shocks the hell out of me. Before I can recover my cool, the waiter's there with our lunches, two salads with blue cheese dressing.

"I see I've rattled your cage," she says, smiling at me, having a good time.

"I felt a little tremor there," I says.

"Let me tell you exactly what I mean by that," Maggie goes on, after, at our say-so, the waiter finishes grinding fresh pepper on the salads and goes away. "There are a lot of people out there who think that because Leo has temporarily lost his power and influence, his wife has done so as well. But my power comes from old money and my influence comes from a network of powerful people, mostly women, that I built and nurtured all by myself. I've used my network to help my husband when I could and if I could, but my network is completely separate from my husband's. Believe it or not, once I learned the game, Leo needed me more than I needed him."

"I'd say he still needs you," I says.

"Now that he's stepped out of the arena? I don't think so. When he gets out I expect he'll hang out at Schaller's Pump in the afternoons telling tales of life inside Washington, holding out his hand to be kissed and making dates with waitresses and the nieces of old cronies."

I detect a little bitterness there, but I don't say anything.

"I suppose you heard the word about Leo and me?" she says.

"I heard rumors about a separation and possible divorce," I says.

"Well, the rumors are true. We've agreed to a legal separation and, when the time seems right, a quiet divorce."

She's watching my reaction. I try not to give one.

"I don't want anything from him. I'll just keep what I already own," she says. "In fact I've agreed to a partnership in case he'd like to set up a consulting firm after he gets out."

"You don't have to tell me any of your personal business," I says.

"Yes, I do, because I want you to know what kind of person I am. There will be a lot of people ready to call me a rat abandoning a ship. A disloyal wife. An opportunist and a climber. I want you to know that I'm none of those things."

"So Leo's got no objections to the separation and divorce?"

She hesitates, takes a bit of salad, a sip on her iced tea.

"A man has his pride," she says. "Even if he wants to call it quits as much as she, it's hard for him to accept if she's the one who suggests it first. It may be doubly difficult because Leo feels the circumstances have taken away much of his ability to fight for the marriage."

"But does he—"

She holds up a hand like she does, cutting me off, telling me she's told me all she wants to tell me. She ain't about to give chapter and verse about her personal life to a man who's no more than an acquaintance. Then she touches my hand, telling me it don't have to stay that way.

"Now will we explore the meaning of the common word I used?"

"I'd rather not," I says.

"I said it to get your undivided attention and to let you know I'm no Georgetown cream puff. So, what do you say? Do you want my help?"

I focus on the fact that what I'm listening to here is an offer of political support. All I got to worry about is what they call the old quid pro quo. Tit for tat. Favor for favor. She just made it pretty clear we can have a little fling or not. My choice.

"I'd like to understand your reasons for the offer a little better," I says.

"Politics is my passion. The same passion you've got."

"I don't think it's the same," I says.

She leans forward, showing me a little of what she's got, her breasts as firm as a girl's twenty years old, the color of milk. But she ain't using them to dazzle or influence me. She's just leaning forward to make sure I hear every word she's got to say.

"It's exactly the same. Exactly. It's not for the money. It's not for the perks. It's simply because you want the power to affect the lives of other people. Even people who'll never meet you, never know you."

"Control," I says.

"The bottom line of practically every human action and

desire. It's all about control. Who's going to hold on to the channel changer when the family's watching TV. Who gets to pick the restaurant even if it means offering to let the other person pick it. Who initiates the phone call."

I smile at that and she smiles right back.

"Everybody thinks it's about money, looting the public treasury," she goes on. "That happens. And it happens that a lot of male politicians use power to score with girls and women. But, bottom line, it's the rush you get when somebody comes to you and asks a favor and you can stick out your finger and punch in a number and get it done."

"Then why don't you run for public office yourself?" I asks.

"I could. I might. But for now all I want is to have discreet access to the levers."

"Be the power behind the throne?"

"Nothing so ambitious, Jim."

So now I'm Jim. She uses the names she calls me according to the kind of relationship she wants me to believe we're forming.

James is a little formal. Old-style good manners. Jim is like we're partners in a common cause. Jimmy's more than old friends, on the way to . . . what?

"All I want is to have a friendly ear, be allowed to ask a question, perhaps make a request now and then, have a place at the table when the pie's getting cut up," she goes on. "I want what everyone who signs a big check to support a charity or a public facility wants, but won't come right out and demand."

She leans back, taking away the invitation that was no invitation, becoming a lady at lunch and not a power broker cutting a deal. She picks up the fork and spears a piece of lettuce, pops it into her pink mouth and smiles at me.

"Eat your salad, Jimmy, it's very good," she says. "There's amaretto chocolate chip cheesecake for dessert. If you want it."

Seven

"How was lunch with Maggie Lundatos?" Mary asks that night while we're sitting down to supper.

"I had a salad."

"What for dessert?"

"They were featuring amaretto chocolate chip cheesecake."

She glances up at me.

"I didn't have any," I says.

She nods and goes back to her plate.

"What to drink?"

"Ginger ale."

She nods again like that answer has some significance.

We ain't talking about what I had for lunch.

"You going out tonight?" she asks.

"I got a call from Cora Esper."

"Do I know her?"

"She was my teacher when I went to night school," I says.

"Maybe you never should've stopped going," Mary says.

"We talked about it and I thought we agreed that I was stretching myself a little too thin."

"You were doing so well," she says.

"I don't think I was doing all that well," I says.

"Well, you weren't saying 'ain't' instead of 'isn't' and 'don't' instead of 'doesn't' as much."

"I try to watch it," I says.

"It takes practice."

"I'll think about it," I says, though why I should think about it I can't tell you.

After all, what with taking over the committeeman's job in the Eleventh and helping whoever takes over for me in the Twenty-seventh, plus the demands made on my time with fixing things around the new house, I'm going to have less time now than I had when we decided I could drop the night school for a while.

Of course that was decided when Mary was still upset about what happened to Pastorelli, one of my fellow students, and still afraid for me, as though going to night school was dangerous.

"Is that all right with you?" I asks.

"If you think about going back to school?"

"Yeah," I says.

"Of course it is."

We're not talking about me going back to school. We're talking about me legitimately going out nights to someplace where Mary can get in touch with me if she needs me.

"What does Cora Esper want?" she asks.

"I got no idea. She left a message on my machine. I tried to call her back but there was no answer. So I thought I'd catch her over to the school where she's still teaching the class I ain't taking anymore."

"See," Mary says.

"See what?"

"You just said ain't."

"Well, I admit I still need help with that."

"You should think about going back to school."

I almost say that I already agreed to do that but I don't. I know how quarrels start.

About this school I was going to. It's what they call the adult extension now. What they used to call night school. I started about three years ago when I took over the job of committeeman in the Twenty-seventh from my old China-man, Chips Delvin—may the Lord bless him and keep him.

I started with two classes then. One in political science and the other in English grammar.

I dropped the political science class, but kept up with the English for another six months after that business with Pastorelli but then I give that up, too.

My punctuation was getting pretty good and my vocabulary had improved, though I got to admit I always had a very good vocabulary. However, though I don't like to say so, I'm having a very hard time with grammar and my pronunciation's also a problem when Mary suggests I take a little time off from self-improvement.

I still say ain't but, come to that, you listen to people with very good educations and they'll say ain't every now and then, just to show everybody that they're regular guys and gals.

My English teacher's this young woman, Cora Esper,

who's married to Jake O'Meara—no relation to Johnny O'Meara—another student I helped out over some business involving a dog he was taking care of under the terms of a will.

I ain't seen much of them since their wedding but when she leaves a message on my machine I decide to go over to the school and catch her in class.

So, at the break, I ask her is everything all right with Jake and she says everything's fine. It's a professional matter that's got her a little upset.

"How can I help?" I asks.

"Have you got any influence with the school board?" she says.

"I know a few people," I says. "And I can always make it my business to meet somebody I'd like to meet. Can you sketch out the situation for me?"

"I teach English at Bochos Elementary full-time. Sixth and seventh grade."

"Is that where you've got the problem?"

"The school board gave me an official reprimand implying that unless I mend my ways my services will no longer be required."

"What's the gist of their complaint?"

"My suggested book list for a program of voluntary reading."

"This ain't . . . isn't . . . the required list?"

"No, I don't change that, though I don't altogether agree with the choices. My reading list is in addition."

"Not instead of?"

"I leave that up to the kids."

"Tell me about this voluntary program."

"Well, you know about the idea Newt Gingrich had

about paying children two dollars a book for every book they read during the summer?"

"He gets a good idea every now and then," I says.

"Well, I started a similar program. Not two bucks, only a dollar, and just for my seventh graders. Even then I had to ask Jake to help me out. He wrote up a little grant proposal and got me some funding."

"How long's the list?"

"I hand out two pages suggesting fifty books, but if any student wants to read a book not on the list, they just have to ask me for an okay. Not because I want to censor what they read but because the first year I tried it one clever kid handed in a list of sixty books he read, not one of which was longer than twenty pages. They were mostly children's picture books."

"You give him the sixty bucks?"

"We negotiated." She grins. "He held out for the whole sixty because he pointed out that he'd discovered a costly flaw in my plan and should be rewarded for helping me plug it up."

"Maybe I should talk to this kid, line him up to be a precinct captain."

"He's got a head on his shoulders, that's for sure."

"So, about the sixty?" I asks again.

"We worked it out I gave him thirty bucks and he came back to me with proof that he read five regular books. He got over on me even then."

"How's that?"

"None of the five were works of fiction or poetry or biography. They were computer manuals."

"I really got to meet this kid," I says.

"I can arrange it, but don't blame me if he cons you out of your wallet."

"They ban the whole list? I mean is the objection that you're putting out an alternate list in the first place?"

"Well, that's what they say I'm supposed to do. Stick with the required list. But the current flap is about just seven books."

"That's a lot."

"That's too much. One would be too much."

"What books did they want removed from your list?" I asks.

"Well, there are the perennial favorites of PTAs and school boards all over the country, *The Adventures of Huckleberry Finn* and Salinger's *Catcher in the Rye*. Steinbeck's *Of Mice and Men* is not acceptable, they say, because of vulgar language, and *Grapes of Wrath* because of that scene where the young woman nurses the starving old man at her breast. Nabokov's *Lolita* is banned because the older man is having a relationship with a young girl. *A Thousand Acres* is unacceptable as well."

"I don't know that last one," I says.

"It won the Pulitzer Prize in 1992."

"What's the objection?"

"It has no literary value for this community at this time."

"Does that mean it might have some literary value later on?" I asks, making a little joke.

Cora shrugs and grins. "You can't get vaguer than they've been about their objections. I don't doubt that most of them haven't even read the books they're banning."

"What else they ban?" I asks.

"*Daddy's Roommate*. It's the most challenged book in

America. That's why I put it on the list, to let the kids make up their own minds about how unacceptable it may be."

"Can I assume that this is a book about a man and woman living together without benefit of wedlock?"

"No, it's about a man and a man living together without benefit of wedlock, which is another contemporary issue that should be argued and examined."

"Uh, oh," I says.

"Would you be offended by a book on the subject, Jimmy?"

"I got to admit I'd need more than a minute to think it through. To paraphrase an old saying, I can decide about the obvious in a lifetime, the subtle takes me a little longer."

When Cora doesn't say anything, I start to explain.

"Oh, I understand," she says. "Just a little book-banning humor there."

"I'll read them two books," I says. "But I'd like to know how important this is to you."

"I'm ready to go to the wall for it, if I have to," she says. "I'm ready to make them fire me."

"If they try to do that, how do you think the Teachers Union'll stand on the issue?"

"I honestly don't know. You know how quickly the support you thought you had can disappear when the going gets tough. You remember what happened during the McCarthy era? All the decent people running for cover? Even Truman and Eisenhower wouldn't or couldn't shut him up."

"Can you get me the names of the board members who voted to ban the books and then voted to censure you?"

"I don't know about the banning but they all voted to censure me. I understand it has to be unanimous."

"A lot of times, over something like this, people'll go along to get along."

"That's the trouble, isn't it, Jimmy?"

"Okay," I says, "I'll see what I can do."

But, right that minute, I ain't got a clue about what I can do.

Eight

Since I became the warlord of the ward, Janet Canarias's been letting me use her storefront office, on selected days and at selected hours, in which to conduct my own ward business. Which is a benefit to her as well as to me.

With Delvin gone and Dunleavy so old I don't think he cares about much except having a nice nap now and then, Janet's become the political person I like to consult when I need to talk something out.

I wouldn't want this taken the wrong way, but the fact that she's a beautiful woman with a preference for members of her own gender when it comes to sex and companionship gives her opinions a very nice balance. I mean we ain't got a lot of politically correct knee-jerk reactions going on when we talk, which keeps a lot of good ideas from getting kicked out the door.

She stops by to pick up some papers on a Monday night and sticks her head in the doorway of my office which used to be a big storage closet with a window.

"No customers, Jimmy?" she says.

"Things've been very peaceful tonight," I says. "You suppose all's right with the Twenty-seventh?"

She makes an eye gesture to the visitor's chair and I nod and smile how pleased I'd be if she'd sit down and chew the fat for a while.

"I'm glad you stopped by," I says. "I was going to come see you."

"A little consultation?" she asks, sitting down and arranging her short skirt over her very pretty thighs.

"I had a meeting with Maggie Lundatos," I says.

She lifts one eyebrow, which is a talent I always admired and which I more or less mastered after a lot of practice in the mirror.

"She was very forthright," I says.

"That's good," she says.

"Put it right out there on the table?"

"It?"

"Her cards, I should've said. What she's ready to give and what she wants for giving."

"Does one depend upon the other?"

"There's no illegal or unethical, or even morally doubtful, quid pro quo here," I says.

"That's quite a legal mouthful there, Jimmy."

"Well I just mean that she's ready to throw her support my way."

"Which is not inconsiderable."

"And all she wants in return is access to the way things work and the opportunity to make a suggestion now and then."

"A suggestion?"

"Which I am not obligated to act upon. I think what she

wants is to learn the ropes. Maybe run for office herself one of these days."

"That was all she had on offer?"

She studies her fingernails as though they was tarot cards and she's about to tell my fortune.

"What do you mean?" I says.

"Is this purely a political consultation, Jimmy?"

"What else do you think it could be?"

"Well, since I believe in alternate lifestyles, you may believe that I'd be more liberal in my views about a person's choice of partners."

"Partners?" I says.

"A person having more than one at a time, for instance."

"You think I want to ask your blessing if I decide to take Maggie Lundatos up on some personal offer?"

"So she made a personal offer?" she says, which is not quite a question but merely a confirmation of what she already suspected.

"Well, it could be just my imagination," I says. "Sometimes, with a woman, it's very hard for a man to know the difference between an invitation or friendliness."

"Don't play coy, Jimmy. You've been hit on plenty, just like I have, and I think you know the difference."

"What makes you say that?"

"Because, as far as I know, your foot hasn't slipped yet and I've been around to witness some of the offers you've had."

I fidget and look at the photo of Delvin at a summer picnic of the Sons of Hibernia held once long ago. I know my cheeks is red.

"Well . . ." I says, which ain't much of a protest.

"It wasn't a condition of her political support, was it?" Janet asks.

"No, it wasn't. She made that clear."

"And how about you, Jimmy? Do you think you might be looking around for some outside interest without even knowing you're looking around?"

I don't say anything.

"You're married . . . what? . . . ten years?" Janet goes on. "Dangerous time in a marriage."

"Seven-year itch?"

"Seven years plus three. Maybe you're overdue wondering about greener grass."

"I don't think so," I says. "But you're right about one thing. It's a woman with what you could call an alternate lifestyle I'd like to talk to you about."

"Not Lundatos?"

"I think I've got my head straight about that," I says. "What would you think if I took Mabel Halstead on as my office manager and administrative aide?"

"My first thought is to find you a gun so you can shoot yourself in the foot."

"What's your second thought?"

"I'd say you couldn't find yourself a better administrator anywhere. You mind telling me what brought her to mind?" she says.

"Well, back when she'd just changed from being a cop by the name of Milton Halstead to a big woman by the name of Mabel Halstead, she stepped into a situation where I could've been severely injured and saved my bacon. You already know what happened when she and Cleary were competing for the middle-aged, middle-class hooker trade. That business about Fay Wray? So I don't have to go into that. But I understand that I brought down so much heat on her, one way and another, that she had to get out of the financial consulting business. So that's why I thought of her to run my office."

"You figure you owe her?"

"I owe her something, but this ain't a case of favor for favor, or even a case of helping somebody I like get into something they might really want to do. I'm being selfish. I want the best person for a job that won't pay too good. If we both get something out of it, that's even better. I understand she's even been talking about really going into politics. Interning over to the state legislature. Maybe doing a summer with a United States representative."

"Yes, she's talking about it."

"Well, maybe this could help her get there."

"There's risk," Janet says. "It gets out you've got a he/she running your office they could use it against you in a nasty way. After all you're not going after a seat in a tenderloin ward. You'll be running in the Mayor's Ward, the Eleventh, maybe the most conservative and Catholic ward in the city."

"So, I'll be giving the voters a chance to show how compassionate and forgiving they can be."

"You ever do anything the easy way, Flannery?" she says.

I give her my best cocky grin.

"One thing," she says.

"Yeah, what's that?"

"Johnny O'Meara's about ready to step down any day, right?"

"I'm waiting for him to name the hour."

"Well, then you better ask him how he'll feel about Mabel."

She gets up, straightens her skirt and goes to the door, which is only three steps away.

"One more thing, Jimmy."

"Yeah?"

"Mary's my best friend next to you. If you decide to do anything about the other half of Maggie Lundatos's offer, I don't want to know about it."

Nine

When I walk into Schaller's Pump, at O'Meara's request, there's a dozen old pols hanging around. They each give me the old one-eye and then they smile, one and all, and say things like, "How's it hangin', Flannery? Tell your old man hello. Tell Mike that Breezy sends his regards," and other such remarks.

O'Meara's sitting in the back at what I see is his usual table, but he ain't alone. He's having a few laughs with these two guys and don't look up until he hears my footsteps approaching them.

Then he says, "Welcome home, Jimmy," and the other two guys look up at me and I recognize these two gazooneys I helped put away in the long ago.

These two is homophobes. One night they get drunk and beat to death two homosexuals who worked in Janet Canarias's campaign, then put them in the steam room of this bathhouse I found to keep Baby, the gorilla, from freezing to death when the heating system in the zoo goes down.

I scare them half to death by trapping them in a cage with

a lion so they give it up with Captain Pescaro standing close enough to hear.

At their trial they put up the old "diminished capacity" defense but what they did is so outrageous and excessive that they get put away for manslaughter . . . ten years. Out in six and a half with good behavior.

Which is not to say that what they did don't go down pretty good with some of the old bigots I know and talk to nearly every day of the week. And which is also not to say that when they get out, there ain't somebody ready, willing and able to give them work. Especially now that they got reputations for being bone-breakers.

They shove their chairs back a little bit when they see it's me and for a second there I'm wondering if I'm going to be in a fight whether I like it or not. But, instead, they grin kind of sheepish and stand up.

"We got no hard feelings, Flannery," Pat Connell says. "I hope you ain't got no hard feelings."

"Hi there, Jimmy. You don't mind I call you Jimmy?" Buck Bailey says.

"Are these special friends of yours, Mr. O'Meara?" I says, not taking my eyes off the two of them. "Because if they are, I won't interrupt your conversation. I'll come back another day."

"They were just chewing the fat with me while I was waiting for you," O'Meara says. "Go ahead, boys. I'll see you around."

They say sure and go on their way, but not before they toss me a couple of looks which shows the hate they got for me under their sheepish smiles.

"Sit down, Jimmy. Have a ginger ale," O'Meara says.

I keep looking after the two gazooneys until they're out the door.

"They're nothing to worry about, Jimmy," O'Meara says.

"I'm not worried about them. I just like to know what they're doing when they're behind my back," I says.

"I understand you had something to do with putting them in the slam."

"I did my best to put them there. My only regret is the law didn't keep them in longer."

"That don't sound like you, Jimmy. I've always been told you're a man of charity and compassion."

"To them what deserves it," I says.

"That may not always be ours to decide," O'Meara says in a voice like a priest in the confessional. "To err is human, to forgive divine. They paid the price and maybe learned a couple of lessons."

When I don't say anything or nod my head in agreement at such wisdom, he goes on. "They're ten years older and their lives in ruin. I figure how about we give them another chance?"

"I can guarantee you, if they don't hurt me or mine, I'm more than happy to keep my hands off them," I says. "But I don't feel so generous about giving them any chances."

"I'm glad to hear you say that you'll keep your hands off them at least. Not interfere should a little bit of good fortune come their way."

This is leading somewhere but I don't ask where. I got this business of him stepping down as committeeman and me being appointed to fill out his term of office to get over with.

"I'm glad you asked for a little sit-down," he says, making it clear that I was the one asked for this meeting though he's the one who called me. "We should hammer out the details of how we're gong to work it, my stepping down, I mean. We can do it with some fanfare, the whole bit, or we can do it quiet and discreet."

"I think I'd like it quiet and discreet," I says.

"Me, too, but Jim Buckey and Maggie Lundatos think otherwise. She said something about the benefits in what you could call a photo opportunity. So, maybe just you and me and Mrs. Lundatos and the chairman in my office and some members of the press. Maybe a few party officials and friends. We don't want you to be accused of being a stealth candidate or a carpetbagger or anything like that."

I can understand what he's saying here. Buckey wants the chance to show that, as the new State Democratic Party Central Committee chairman, he's inherited the clout that Ray Carrigan once exercised. Like naming committeemen to fill out terms of them what retire midterm not being the least important.

Maggie wants to take the first chance she can get to show that Maggie Lundatos, now that she's ending her marriage as well as her political ties with Lundatos, is now a player in her own right.

O'Meara wants his favor to me and the party to be as public as he can make it. Retired he may be but out of the game altogether he ain't.

"How about my office?" I asks.

"Your office is over in the Twenty-seventh, ain't it? Well, that wouldn't look so good, would it, pointing up to the fact that you're bailing out of a minority ward to sit yourself down in my butter tub?"

There's always this edge to whatever O'Meara says to me. Like there's more than a little bit of disdain for me, a man who climbed the ladder so far without the trouble of running for any office. A little bit of dislike, too. And, maybe, a little bit of envy.

"I think you're right," I says. "How about your office?"

"How about right here at Schaller's?" he says. "Let the old boys taste a little of what it was like in the good old days. We'll have a beer bust."

"I wasn't thinking about anything fancy."

"Me neither. The Pump ain't got much that's fancy to offer. Just friends and family is all. So, how about I set it up for next Wednesday night? Invite a couple of people. Your old man and your wife at least. Maybe some of the people you're gong to want in your new organization."

"There's someone I'd like to invite but I wanted to ask you first."

"You don't need my permission," he says, pleased that I asked.

"I wasn't going to ask permission," I says. "I just want to keep you informed."

"So who did you have in mind?"

"You remember Milton Halstead, used to be a cop?"

"I don't think I know anyone by that name."

"You remember Lou Cleary, also a cop?"

"Him, I think I know. Works for his son-in-law, Jack Diversey, the undertaker? Also works as an agent for some professional ladies."

"He quit that business," I says.

O'Meara grins, not giving what I said any notice. "Oh, yeah," he says. "He provided a few sweethearts for a smoker we run over at the Sons of Hibernia." Then he quickly adds, "I, however, though tempted, did not partake."

"Well, this Halstead, who now calls himself Mabel, gave him a little competition."

"I remember now. It was going around City Hall. This he/she had some scheme about stock portfolios, health plans and other financial matters."

"That he/she is very much a she, no matter how she might have started out," I says.

"This Halstead a special friend of yours?"

He makes it sound like there's something nasty going on between us.

"She's the person I want to be my office manager and principal aide."

"You need an office manager I can get you a half a dozen great women who'll do you a job. Also the same if you think you need an aide."

Again there's the double meaning and the little smirk.

"I'm more or less looking for someone I can trust," I says. "Somebody I know can do the job." I give my reply a little twist, talking his language, letting him think anything he wants to think.

"Well, I'm not the sort of man sticks his nose into another man's private business," he says. "What you do is what you do. But, if you'll take a little piece of advice from an older man, I'd keep this lady friend of yours as far in the back office as you can. Don't let her hang around the water cooler, if you know what I mean."

Ten

On Monday I go down to the Board of Education and ask to talk to somebody about the way the school boards work.

The receptionist asks me am I asking because I'm interested in running for one of the school councils.

"How many councils is there?" I asks.

"Five hundred and thirty-nine," she says. "In which one would you be interested?"

"Well, I suppose I'm interested in Bochos Elementary."

"Are you a parent, a teacher or a community activist?"

"Well actually I'm the Democratic ward leader in the Twenty-seventh Ward, soon to be, maybe, the ward leader in the Eleventh."

"Can you do that, be the leader in two wards?" she asks.

She's got these big brown eyes which she fixes on my mouth and won't let go except occasionally looking at my eyes. I wonder is she a lip-reader.

"Actually, I'll resign from the Twenty-seventh when I take up my duties at the Eleventh."

"Will you have to resign from the Twenty-seventh before

you become the leader of the Eleventh or the other way around?"

"I never thought about it," I says. "It's all sort of informal except O'Meara wants to have a celebration when he retires and hands the Eleventh to me over to Schaller's Pump."

"He can do that?"

"Do what?"

"Just hand the leadership of a ward over to you?"

"Actually Jim Buckey, the chairman of the State Democratic Central Committee, will have to appoint me to fill out O'Meara's term of office."

"It's all very casual, isn't it?" she says. "The way offices are tossed around in this city."

"You're not from this city?"

She gives me this big smile and says, "Born and raised in the Tenth, but I live out in Evanston now." Then she picks up a pen and says, "You'll want to talk to Ms. Shute, the Information officer. Who shall I say?"

"Jimmy Flannery."

"I've heard of you," she says. "When I was a little girl you did something nice for Baby, the gorilla."

"You remember that?" I says, feeling good that she should remember such a thing.

"Oh, I do, I do," she says, and smiles again.

She pushes a couple of buttons on a small console. Somebody picks up right away. She murmurs my name and background, then hangs up and says to me, "Right down the hall to the right, third door on the left. Ms. Shute."

By the time I get to the right office, Ms. Shute is standing there waiting to usher me in.

I think to myself that this is a person out to make an impression. This is an organization out to make sure they got the best public relations they can have. Which tells me two things. One that they're having some difficulty with some portion of the citizens. And, two, I ain't been keeping up with the doings down at the Board of Education.

"Please sit down, Mr. Flannery," Ms. Shute says, as she walks me across a floor which is carpeted in industrial grade wall to wall, evidence of their frugality. There's also a little Oriental rug which I'm sure she bought and put down to add a little color to the drab gray.

"I understand you're the Democratic Party ward leader in the Twenty-seventh, soon to be the leader in the Eleventh," she says.

"I was explaining to that nice young woman at reception that I won't be holding both jobs simultaneously."

She holds up a hand. "I understand. Are you interested in the school councils for yourself or one of your constituents?"

"For a friend."

"Yes?" she says, waiting, I think, for a name.

"She doesn't know I'm here to see you," I says. "She hasn't given me permission to use her name. So, for right now, I think I'll just keep it to myself, you don't mind. But I should add that, now that she's got me interested, there's a lot I'd like to know for myself."

"About what?"

"About how things are going since the governor gives the mayor unusual powers to reorganize the educational system."

"You're aware of that, then?" she says.

"Well, I read the papers and watch the news on television," I says. "Also things like this get talked about when you've got an interest in politics."

"You know why the governor gave the mayor such unusual powers over the Board of Education?" she asks.

"I understand that back at the beginning of the eighties there was this school engineer by the name of Marty Conracky controlled the contracts for all repair work in the high schools in Chicago. His brother, George, owned three companies specializing in heating, air-conditioning, electrical and plumbing, and so forth. These brothers ran a scheme to overcharge, marking repairs and replacement parts up as much as eighty percent when the purchasing rules already allowed them a very generous thirty percent profit."

She nods, giving me an A for scholarship.

"That was just one case of malfeasance and misfeasance," she says.

"And also downright fraud and thievery," I says.

"They'd call it highway robbery in Streets and Sanitation," she says, and smiles.

We're exchanging little jokes here.

"Multiply the Conracky situation by a hundred and you have a vague idea of how corrupt officials and contractors conspired to get rich while the schools fell down around the children's ears," she says.

"So Governor Jim Edgar gives the mayor unprecedented powers to turn the city school system around and sweep out the stables."

"He did. And Mayor Daley appoints the man who cleaned up City Hall chief operating officer of the district. The first audit revealed a million dollars in spoiled food, tuna, eggs, canned fruit, and other stuff . . . some of it with expiration dates fifteen years old."

"Didn't it also uncover an employee who was stealing rolls of toilet paper and selling them to a local discount store?" I says.

"You're well informed, Mr. Flannery."

"I try to keep up, Ms. Shute. And please call me Jimmy."

"Mrs. I don't insist on Ms. any longer."

"Why not?"

"It was getting burdensome. Like switching over to metric from decimal. But, actually, I'd rather you call me Helen, Jimmy."

"Thank you, Helen. So has there been improvement with this new arrangement?"

"We've restructured the phone system contracts and saved the city over two million dollars. We've laid off more than seventeen hundred employees, many of them relatives of ex–board members and politicians."

"Ain't you also had to station security cops and metal detectors at every entrance to the three-block central service area in the Near West Side for fear some disgruntled person does a PO?"

"A PO?"

"For 'post office.' A person appearing at their former place of employment with an automatic weapon in their hands, firing from the hip at one and all."

A little frown appears on her forehead, between her eyes.

"There will always be some trouble and discontentment when a great many changes are made all at once," she says.

"But armed guards are a little much," I says.

"Reasonable precautions until things settle down," she says.

"I understand you've had some clashes with school councils," I says, feeding her more of what I read up on before I came to see her.

"It was necessary to dissolve the council at Parker High School after investigating charges of teacher intimidation, misappropriated money and grade fixing," she says, getting a little wary.

"Yeah? And didn't you have a council member at Jameson Elementary wear a mike to catch an interim principal offering bribes to council members in order to win approval of a permanent contract of employment?"

"Yes, there was that unfortunate incident as well."

"Did you dissolve that council, too?"

She don't know where I'm going with any of this but she's sure that I'm finally where I was going from the beginning of the interview. There's a little chilling of her manner.

"No," she says. "Just those implicated in the bribery."

"Can you tell me how many people there are on each of these local councils?"

"They are made up of six parents, two community members at large and two teachers."

"And, you don't mind telling me, what are their responsibilities and duties?"

"They have the power to hire and fire principals, prepare school budgets and improvement plans."

"How about books? Choosing books for the children's reading?"

"The councils have a very strong voice in what kind of books will be shelved in the school library and what supplemental reading will be okayed," she says, leaving me with the uncomfortable feeling that she's about to exercise what they call plausible deniability if I start making unpleasant accusations.

"You ever interfere with any of these councils if you think any of them is applying undue censorship?" I asks.

She smiles one of them superior little smiles people who consider themselves experts smile. "To determine what constitutes undue censorship would seem to be as difficult as determining which books were to be allowed and which not allowed in school libraries. Wouldn't you say?"

"You got a point there. But I'd say you acted swiftly enough when it came to putting wires on civilians and firing school councils wholesale."

"Now it's my turn to concede your point. I may be consulted but I do not, finally, make policy."

"That would be?"

"Mr. Lloyd Moraine."

"You think I could see him?"

"I'm sure you could, but not at the moment. His wife, Mary, just underwent surgery and he's at the hospital."

"I'm sorry to hear that."

"I could check his calendar and make an appointment for you, but I can't even be sure how chaotic that calendar will be for the next several weeks or so."

"Could you tell me where Mr. Moraine lives?"

She hesitates for half a second, weighing the dangers of giving a stranger the home address of her boss.

"I could look it up," I says. "It's a matter of public record."

"Sangamon Street," she says, giving me half a loaf.

"In Bridgeport?"

She nods her head.

"You got a street number?"

She gives it to me.

"Just three or four blocks from where I live," I says, and that seems to make her feel better.

Before I go I reach out to shake her hand and I says, "I can see I need to talk to Mr. Moraine but I don't want to leave you in the dark. I got reason to believe the council over to Bochos is throwing their weight around when it comes to what books can and can't be read by their students. You've got no reason to mind if I object to that kind of censorship, do you, Helen?"

"No, I do not, Jimmy," she says.

We're friends again.

Eleven

The next day I call Mabel and make a date to meet her at Cricket's. I get there before she does and I'm sitting there when she walks in and pauses in the entrance. She's wearing white panty hose under a short tartan skirt with a white blouse and a tartan jacket to match the skirt. She's tossed another piece of plaid over her shoulder so it ain't quite a sash, yet not quite a shawl. Tall as she is, everybody looks her over as though there's a new queen in town. She spots me and comes striding on over, long-legged and sure of herself.

I think that she still walks a little like a cop crossing a barroom floor.

On the other hand that's probably the way confident ladies over six feet tall walk nowadays.

She slides into the chair the maître d' holds for her and flashes him a smile and a silent thank you.

"I'm the envy of every guy in the joint," I says in a low voice, wondering what's the best way to compliment a woman friend who was once a man

"If they only knew."

"Then I'd be the envy of every woman too."

She grins. "I don't do mixed parties, Jimmy."

"I wasn't suggesting . . ." I says, feeling flustered.

She reaches across the table and slaps me on the wrist.

We order and the waiter goes away.

"This an occasion?" Mabel says.

"I hope it's a celebration," I says.

"Janet said you had a proposition to put to me."

"Huh," I says, never being at a loss for a quick reply.

"The world's full of double entendres, isn't it?" she says. "What's the offer?"

"To be my office manager after I'm named committeeman of the Eleventh and my chief aide after I become alderman. There won't be much money at first, but later on we'll talk about something permanent that'll pay a lot more than I can pay you now."

"You come right to the point, don't you, Jimmy?"

"I don't like to shuffle the cards too long," I says. "I like to get them right out there on the table."

"Have you thought this through?"

"Yes, I have."

"All the way through?"

"Every step of the way. I know you for a long time now."

"Ever since I was Milton."

"You were a man and a cop everybody could trust. That ain't changed no matter what else has changed. So, I want somebody I can completely trust at the heart of my organization. Also you already proved, with your financial package scheme for the ladies, that you're one hell of an administrator."

She nods, acknowledging the compliment, taking it as her due.

"You've got City Hall smarts, street smarts and people smarts," I go on. "How could I do better?"

"You probably couldn't. What are you talking about an organization for? The party's your organization, isn't it? They're handing these jobs to you, aren't they?"

"Yes, they are. I'm not so worried about retaining the committeeman's job when I got to run for it. But I'm not so sure I won't have plenty of competition when I have to defend the alderman's seat. I ain't got a strong background and a ton of friends in the Eleventh like I do in the Twenty-seventh, so I can't be positive they won't bounce me for a neighbor first chance they get. Like you just pointed out, whatever I got so far has been handed to me and that's why I need people like you around me to make sure I can earn what I been given."

She lays her hand on me and it's the soft hand of a woman. "Oh, no, Jimmy," she says. "You worked for everything you've got. You earned it."

"I thank you for that," I says.

"I'd be proud to run your office."

"You understand—" I start to say, but she cuts me off.

"I understand I can't be there out front. I'm carrying a lot of baggage you don't need."

"That ain't what I was going to say," I says. "I ain't going to hide you in no closet. You already come out of it big-time and I ain't going to dishonor you in any way."

"According to a lot of people, many of whom are the people you're hoping will support you when the time comes, I'm worse than a fallen woman. I'm a fallen *it*. A fallen unmentionable. The political climate the country's in, it's not enough that the candidate's clean. Everybody around him, including the boy who shines his shoes, has to be politically correct."

"Maybe that's why I'm asking you," I says. "I been walking through other people's shit for a good part of my life, so it don't bother me if I'm walking against the tide."

"You're not just using me to make a point?"

"I don't think so, but I can't be sure. You think I'm using you that way?"

"No, though I wouldn't mind if some people got the message. Live and let live."

"How hard is it? How bad does it get?" I asks.

"Very hard and very bad. I meet a new man and I like him. Somewhere along the line, sooner rather than later, I've got to make a decision about sex.

"Do I come right out and say that I lived life as a man, a cop, for most of my life? And if that's okay with him, then it means I start to think that maybe I've got somebody kinky on my hands instead of a very, very mature understanding guy."

"That's working against yourself," I says.

"I can't help myself thinking the way I think any more than the average man can stop thinking the way he thinks after I give him the news. From the point of view of a good many . . . most . . . of them, they're about to make love to a person of the same sex. And what does that make him?"

She goes silent and I don't have a thing to say. So we sit there staring at the tablecloth for a minute, maybe hoping to find some answers or something there.

"You ever regret it?" I finally says.

"I'd be lying if I said that there were never times when I wish I'd never had the operation. That I wish that I was still Milton the cop, telling dirty jokes and drinking beer with the other cops. That kind of easy friendship can be more satisfying than sex sometimes. But then I remember the discomfort . . . no, the pain . . . I suffered feeling that I wasn't what I appeared to be. Feeling that I was a woman trapped in an alien body."

"So, you think us men is aliens?" I says, trying to make a little joke there, afraid that the conversation's getting way too glum.

The lunch comes.

Milton grins this beautiful white-teeth-and-red-lipstick grin at me.

"You think a sixteen-ounce steak is too much for a light lunch?" Mabel asks in a confidential tone of voice.

"You're a very big girl," I says.

"I promise you I won't expect the same every time we have lunch together," she says, and dives right in.

Twelve

So I keep putting together a staff, keeping it lean and mean, not loading it up with honorary titles and too many chiefs.

I ask my father to be my campaign manager.

"Ain't it a little early to be worrying about a campaign manager?" he says. "Everything goes the way it's supposed to go, you won't have to defend the seat until '99."

"There's an awful lot of people I got to meet and an awful lot of things I got to learn before '99. It'll roll around quicker than you think."

He stares at me like I just reminded him of something he almost forgot. I know what it is. He's thinking that '99 might seem only a little ways off to me but it's only a blink of an eye to him. He's thinking that he might not even be around to participate in any campaign when '99 rolls around.

He hugs me and says, "No thanks, sonny," which he hardly ever calls me. "You want a campaign manager," he says, "you should go talk to Aunt Sada, the Socialist.

"Now don't get me wrong. I ain't copping out altogether.

When the time comes, I'll be out there knocking on doors, don't you worry about that. I'll walk the neighborhoods with you if I got the steam. And you better not include me out of any strategy sessions. I still got a couple ideas, you know?"

Aunt Sada colors up when I ask her to run my campaign, she's so pleased with me asking.

Then she asks, "But are you sure it's such a good idea?"

"Why's it not a good idea?"

"Well, it's come to my attention that this woman who was once a man . . ."

"Mabel Halstead. Yeah?"

"She's going to run your office and be your right hand. It's already a well-known fact that your closest political ally is Janet Canarias, a beautiful woman who prefers other women over men."

"Uh-huh?"

"It's also a well-known fact that your principal backer is Margaret Lundatos, soon to be ex-wife of a man in prison."

"She's not bailing out on him because he's doing time," I says.

"You don't have to defend her. I understand she just thought it was time to do what she'd probably been planning to do for a long time. In fact, I think if he'd been able to stay free and active in politics, she would've stuck by him and accommodated his ambitions. But what we're talking about when '99 comes around is a divorced woman backing a politician running for office in a predominantly Catholic ward."

I half hear what she says after telling me I didn't have to defend Maggie. I sort of got stuck right there.

"Was I defending her?" I asks.

"That's what it sounded like to me. But that's not really important. What's important is you're putting together a staff that's all women who are not quite all women. That's still no guarantee you'll attract the feminine vote, but you're sure as hell going to lose the bigots and chauvinists."

"I'm not sure I want them votes," I says.

"Then prepare to lose. Everybody gives lip service to liberality but underneath it all we're all riddled with prejudices. I'm not telling you to turn your back on your friends or your principles. I'm just saying you're going to want a more even mix of straight and gay, male and female, conservative and liberal on your team. This isn't your home neighborhood we're talking about."

"After you come aboard, Aunt Sada, I'll take on nobody but monsignors in the Catholic Church and the presidents of banks."

"What makes you think monsignors are conservative?"

A note comes to me from Maggie Lundatos.

There's no opening salutation, my name don't appear.

It says, "Thank you for accepting my offer. I'll be working for you in the background. Enclosed is a check. I would like you to consider taking Robert Shaftoe on your staff as an unpaid volunteer. He would like to meet with you at your convenience and may be reached at this number." Which she's got written down. Then she adds, "You need a man to balance all the women."

I'm wondering if this is a little test, taking on a staff member I don't know, haven't even met. A little quid pro quo. Favor for favor, Chicago style. I've got no reason to say no but I don't say yes.

The note goes on to say "Love" but that could just be the usual closing salutation.

The note's unsigned.

The check's a cashier's check drawn on Carteret Enterprises, a leasing company, owned by Maggie Lundatos. It's for five thousand dollars and is signed by the company's financial officer, one Robert Shaftoe.

I get the feeling that Maggie's building her own political organization early in the game.

I send the check back with an unsigned, typewritten note of my own saying that my campaign policy will be not to accept more than one thousand dollars from an individual and one hundred from a corporation, organization or institution.

I also say I would love to meet Robert Shaftoe and invite her to bring him along to Schaller's Pump that coming Friday night . . . O'Meara having called me with a change of date because Friday and Saturday nights are the nights when you can expect the biggest crowds to any given event . . . when O'Meara's going to announce his resignation as the committeeman in the Eleventh and Jim Buckey'll announce my appointment to finish out O'Meara's term of office.

But first, I go down to City Hall and bend the knee or kiss the ring . . . whichever way you want to put it . . . since the mayor won't be at Schaller's Pump, having a lot better things to do than witness the elevation of a sewer inspector to the position of warlord in the Mayor's Ward.

When his secretary shows me in, he stands up from behind the big old scarred desk, hand outstretched, big smile on his open Irish kisser, running the facts about who I am and what I want through his head, tickling the file, looking so much like his old man that it's like I'm watching an old newsreel or TV clip.

"It's very good to see you again, Jim. Tell me, how's your father?"

"He groans a little when he gets up out of a chair," I says, taking the chair the mayor's offering to me with a wave of his hand.

"Don't we all, now and again," he says, pulling back his shoulders a little, a natural-born politician showing the world how strong and vigorous he is.

He sits down. "A fireman, wasn't he?"

"In the Fourteenth."

"That's right. My father always spoke fondly of your father."

That might well have been the truth, but I doubted it would've indicated a special fondness. It's a politician's gift. A talent for remembering names and faces. An ability that is dying out, I think, along with all the other feats of memory required before speed dialers and storage devices of a hundred kinds came along to remember things for us. It's even hard for me to remember Aunt Sada's phone number. I want to call her I just punch in one number on my telephone's keypad.

"How can I help you?" the mayor asks.

"You sent word that you wanted to see me," I says.

He snaps his fingers.

"You're taking O'Meara's seat as alderman."

"No, sir. I'm going to fill out his term as committeeman in the Eleventh."

"That's right. It always interests me how one retirement or one death of an officeholder creates a hundred opportunities and challenges down the line. This time you're the beneficiary of an improvement in your position, plus you have the opportunity to see the chance you had passed on to another."

He stands up and reaches out his hand for another quick squeeze.

I'm out of there.

He don't even walk me to the door.

Thirteen

The next day this skinny, ginger-haired young guy finds me at my desk down in the Sewer Department.

He's got this easy grin and reminds me a little bit of the young Jack Kennedy, with those faraway, squinty eyes you get from doing a lot of sailing and things like that.

"Hi, my name's Robert Shaftoe," he says, sticking out his hand and grinning.

"How'd you find me?" I asks.

"I asked around and was told that you're one public servant who puts in his nine-to-five every day of the week." He puts in a little beat there. "Except sometimes."

"Have a seat," I says, letting go his hand. "You want I should get you something?"

He sees the coffeepot on the table in back of me and says, "I can pour my own. Would you like me to pour you one as well?"

"I'm sort of coffeed out," I says.

"Come to think of it, so am I," he says, and settles back in the chair as though he's giving me his undivided attention.

He dips his hand into the breast pocket of his jacket and comes out with some folded sheets of paper, which he hands over to me.

"My CV," he says.

"What?"

"Curriculum vitae."

I unfold the sheets . . . there's three of them . . . and start reading.

"Robert Bartlett Shaftoe."

Then there's his address and phone number. From the apartment number I can see he lives in a flat in Uptown in the Forty-eighth.

"Born 1962." So he's thirty-five. "Arlington, Virginia."

He got out of grammar school in '73, middle school in '76 and high school in '79.

"Army brat," he says.

"What's that?"

"Bouncing from school to school, city to city and state to state," he says.

"You went back to Virginia for your college though," I says.

"Virginia Military Academy," he says. "Family tradition that goes back to the Civil War. Long line of Shaftoes in the service of the nation."

"But you didn't make a career out of the army."

"But I did go into public service for a while. You can see there."

"CIA?"

"Nothing exciting. I was just a glorified file clerk," he says.

I didn't believe that. On the other hand I didn't believe he was out there doing secret, dangerous things, either. I notice, talking to these intelligence agency types, that they make little of what they did with the intention of making you think they were shooting spies in the eye and diving out of airplanes into some impenetrable jungle somewheres you ain't even heard of.

"Why'd you quit?"

He shrugs, smiles and shakes his head as though I'm getting into a sensitive area.

Then he says by way of explanation, "I was tired of being a file clerk."

"You wanted action?"

"Well, not a shooting war. I just wanted the opportunity to see things happen."

"So you went to work for Senator Harlan," I says, reading from the page.

"I served as his aide for two years. Ninety-three and '94. Exciting times. The Republican revolution. Gingrich."

"How'd you connect with Maggie Lundatos?"

"Senator Moseley-Braun naturally wanted to be informed of all ongoing congressional investigations. I did most of the legwork."

"Into Leo Lundatos?"

"Among others."

"CIA training?" I says, and give him one of his friendly grins.

He gives it to me right back. "It comes in handy from time to time. Not many people know how to be as discreet as I know how to be."

"So, it says here that you left the senator's employ in '95. Did Lundatos give you an offer you couldn't refuse?"

"Something like that. He was under attack and needed everything he could get to defend himself."

"By digging up some dirt on his enemies to use as bargaining pieces?"

"Know thine enemies," Shaftoe says, not even making it sound self-righteous. "Is there anything I can do?"

I got a half a dozen books on my desk, some of the ones the Bochos Elementary School council banned, some of which I bought and some of which I got out of the library. Reading them is on my list of things to do but it's very hard for me to find the time.

"You could read these and tell me what you think."

He's another eyebrow raiser. Up one eyebrow goes.

He checks the titles.

"*Huckleberry Finn?*" he says. "*A Thousand Acres.* Pulitzer Prize winner, wasn't it?"

"You know it?"

"Not this particular one." He looks in the front of the book. "Published '90, '91. That means it would've won its prize in '92."

He picks up the next book. "*Daddy's Roommate,*" he reads off the cover, and snaps me the eyebrow again.

"You know that one, too?" I asks.

"Heard of it. Didn't win any prizes though. Say, you don't mind my asking?"

"Go ahead."

"You doing some book reports for night school classes? Something like that?"

I give him a quick sketch of the situation over to Bochos Elementary.

"I'm going over there tonight when they have their school council meeting."

"You know most of these book-banning scares are nothing but smoke and mirrors," he says.

"How's that?"

"Well, practically every day some public interest group in D.C. or elsewhere puts out another fifty-page report. The reporters, who may be ... or at least consider themselves ... seriously overworked, read the conclusions first and if they seem credible, there's a great temptation to just skim the rest of it. Maybe condense the first page and the last page, stick in a data table, if called for, and file the story. There's one outfit puts out an annual report called 'Attacks on the Freedom to Learn' which always prompts hundreds of stories in the press around the country. It's all about which books have been banned and where the banning took place."

"Sort of like *Forbes* putting out the issue on how much people make or the magazines what put out surveys of the places to live?" I says, sticking my oar in.

"Like that," he says. "It's filler and produces a lot of letters to the editor."

"So, are you saying these books ain't really been banned?"

"Oh, they've been banned, all right. Everybody gets upset. Mostly because the report always says that censorship is getting worse each and every year. It attracts the attention of people like the ACLU and the National Library Association's Freedom Committee. Also, it attracts a lot of grant money."

"Oops," I says.

He's just put us on the beginning of the money trail, which is many times the real reason why people and organizations get involved in causes.

I wonder if there's a money angle here.

Shaftoe grins again. He knows I'm ahead of him or at least right alongside.

"That's right," he says. "The way it works is these people

who make the reports know the reporters want to duck all the legwork they can, unless it's a Watergate. They know that if you print a scary story it'll get printed. You spend a year working on a document that looks like it was researched up the ying-yang, knowing that the reporters will assume that it lives up to rigorous standards."

"Which it don't?"

"Which it practically never does."

"That's it? That's the smoking gun? There ain't really any censorship and book banning to speak of?"

"Oh, there's always some. How can there not be, people worried about seeing that their kids don't get their hands on the wrong stuff? Books are banned. It happens and it shouldn't, but there's not near as much as they say there is.

"For instance, the most banned book in America, which is usually *Of Mice and Men* when it's not *Huckleberry Finn*, has about a dozen complaints against it every year in the public schools, of which there are about eighty thousand. Of those complaints, most never get farther than the school librarian. Sometimes the books are restricted for the lower grades but that's about as far as it goes."

"How do you know all this?"

"I'm one of those people," he says.

"One of what people?"

"One of those people with a memory that sweeps up everything I read."

I'm thinking that Maggie has sent me a very valuable addition to my staff, such as it is at the moment.

"Also," he goes on, "I worked for People for the American Way for about a year."

"Watchdog group?" I asks.

"Watchdog group," he says. "But you'll have to trust me when I tell you they're very legitimate."

"How come you ain't got that listed in your résumé?"

"It was pro bono volunteer work."

"Well, this complaint I got is on my plate and I can't ignore it. So, if you'll read them and give me a rundown, so I'll sound like I know what I'm talking about when I go confront a certain person, I'd be obliged."

"Happy to do it," he says, picking up the books and leaving the office with a wave of his hand.

I sit there wondering if Maggie's handed me a jewel or, like they say, planted a viper in my bosom.

Fourteen

I go sit in the back of the classroom over to Bochos Elementary, which is in SuHu on the Near North Side in the Eighth Ward, where the school council is meeting.

They ain't arrived yet. I pick up an agenda, with the names of the members on it, at the table up front and go back to my seat to read it.

There's Jane Roberts and Michael Hunger, the teachers, and the Reverend Stephen Arbori, pastor of the First Southern Baptist Church, and Johnson Foraker, retired customs officer, the at-large members of the community.

Then we got the parents, four mothers and two fathers.

One name seems familiar to me but I can't exactly place from where I know it. Of course, in a city the size of Chicago there's got to be duplications everywhere.

By the time a quorum has arrived there's only three other people in the audience.

When they call the roll call, the teachers and the at-large members are all there, but only three of the parents are in attendance. Harriet Finn, Phillip Pelham and Sheila Weiss are absent.

Present are Mrs. O'Leary, Mrs. Sturges, and this guy, Joseph Asbach, the one with the name I thought I heard before. Which I did hear before, more than once, more than twice.

More than ten years ago I tangled with this gazooney. He's rousing the rabble and staging protest marches, mostly with protestors he buys for a five-dollar bill. I meet him after a bomb goes off and kills a couple of innocent people over to the abortion clinic on Sperry. After some pretty powerful people come to his aid, I'm never able to prove he had a hand in it.

I keep my eyes, ears and nose out for news of him all these years but he drops out of sight and I figure he's moved his act elsewhere. Now here he is back again. First Connell and Bailey, the bone-breakers, and now Asbach, the bomber.

The years ain't been bad to him. They've pared his face down to the bone and he's lost some hair so he's got one of them widow's peaks. His skin's very pale. He looks a little like a poet who's suffered a lot.

His eyes are set back in his head, what you might call brooding. He's still a very good-looking character, if you don't look too close into them brooding eyes.

He recognizes me too. He stares at me and gives me a little bit of the curly lip, at which he's very good.

There's maybe twenty minutes before the meeting's supposed to start. He gets up and comes walking over to me.

"I hope you're not going to step on my shoeshine again," he says, reminding me of the way I greeted him years ago.

"It looks like you ain't going to give me the chance," I

says, glancing down at his Reebok running shoes. "You still active in the anti-choice movement?"

"The way you politicians use the language," he says, like he's disgusted and amused. "You're pro-abortion. You're for killing the unborn. But the way you state the position makes me out to be a narrow-minded bigot denying people the right to make their own decision."

"That sums it up," I says.

"So, while you're insisting that women should have the right to murder their babies, you're telling me I don't have the right to protest it. Is that correct?"

"Not when you preach violence."

"Have you forgotten that charges were never brought against me?"

"You had friends."

He shrugs as though he's had enough of me.

"You've come a long way, Flannery. I see you're a ward leader."

"I am."

"Then you must have a lot more on your plate than when you were a precinct captain walking the sewer pipes. You must have enough to do in your own ward to keep you busy and not interfere in the business of the Eighth."

"A friend asked me to look in on your meeting. How about you, Asbach, what have you been doing?"

"Minding my business, which I'm suggesting is what you should do."

"I see you're a parent on this council."

"My child lived. It wasn't aborted."

"So you got married. I thought you liked to frolic with ladies for hire."

"It's none of your business but for some reason, unknown

to me, I feel I want you to understand that I act upon princi-
ple and not self-aggrandizement. You understand what I'm
saying?"

"I understand the words," I says. "I ain't sure I understand
the meaning."

"I had a relationship with a young lady. Our precautions
failed and she became pregnant. She was going to have an
abortion."

"Didn't you offer to marry her?"

"I did, but she didn't wish to marry me. She had, she said,
a great deal of life still to live before she settled down to dull
domesticity. I allowed she had the right to refuse marriage
but not to get rid of my child. I insisted she have the baby
and I arranged to take custody a week after she was born."

"So you had a girl?"

For the first time his face relaxes and a look comes in his
eyes. I can see the feeling he has for his daughter.

"How old is she?" I asks.

"Six."

"That's my baby's age," I says.

He starts to give me a little smile, one father to another,
but grabs it back like he's afraid it'll make us friends.

"What is it your friend wanted you to do?" he asks.

"Seems there's somebody banning books around here."

"There you go, using excessive language again," he says,
shaking his head and smiling the way Reagan did that time
he wiped the floor with Jimmy Carter. "I'd prefer to say that
there are some of us who are trying to protect our children—those that are allowed to be born—from filthy and
degrading books."

"I don't even have to ask," I says. "You're the leader of the
vigilantes."

"There you go again," he says, repeating that famous Reagan line. "Twisting language."

All of a sudden I realize that he's right. I'm walking in there with my own set of prejudices. My mind's made up before I even hear the arguments for and against. I'm about to say so when he smirks at me and says, "Excuse me, I got to go take a pee before I do it on your shoe."

The meeting's as dull as these meetings usually are. But, fortunately, it don't last long.

When it's over, I don't wait around to trade any more remarks with Asbach but go out into the dark parking lot and get into my car.

As I'm driving out into the road, this big Chrysler sedan comes whipping around in front of me, its motor banging away.

It's Asbach behind the wheel and he gives me the finger.

"Ah, you silly sonofabitch," I says to myself. "You better get the cylinders on that goddam hearse fixed."

Fifteen

Last year Frank O'Shea, the bad cop in the good cop/bad cop routine of Rourke and O'Shea, invites me to his daughter's wedding. Which, in the first place, comes as a great surprise to me since he insults me every chance he gets and threatens me when he's not insulting me. In the second place, he tells me his daughter and future son-in-law agreed to a very small wedding and a reception with only family and a few close friends invited. I never knew he considered me a friend let alone a close one.

"I convinced my wife and the kids that it's very foolish to piss away five thousand, six thousand dollars on the church and reception when we can do it sweet and simple for maybe a thousand and they can pocket the rest to start their household," he explains to me while we're standing around looking at this body of a bookie found in a betting parlor in my ward.

"You're ready to hand them a check for five very large?" I asks, bowled over by his generosity.

"Well, twenty-five hundred," he says, satisfied that he's not only doing good by them but by his wallet, too.

But, in the actuality, the wedding and reception plans get away from him, the way it's got away from ninety percent of the fathers of daughters with which I am acquainted.

When I arrive at the church it's full to busting and at the reception in Shamrock Gardens it looks like half the Irish in Chicago are swilling beer and scarfing up the cold cuts, not to mention the Italians, Poles, Bohemians, Jews and African Americans from both sides of the criminal divide who have come into contact with O'Shea over the years.

So that's how it hits me when I walk into the hall upstairs over Schaller's Pump where the little ceremony of retirement and appointment is supposed to take place with maybe twenty people, tops, attending.

Mary don't come with me, her interest in politics, nowadays, extending only to my participation in it. She's more than happy to avoid any of the public contact it requires of wives except when it's absolutely necessary.

But that don't mean I arrive alone. Aunt Sada's on one arm and Mabel Halstead's on the other. My old man's walking right in front of me, like he's parting the crowd, looking grand, old as he is. Shaftoe, smiling like he's the candidate, is behind me angled off to the right.

Buck Bailey spots me and shoulders his way through the crowd with this big grin on his kisser. I don't like it because I don't know how to play it. Here's a gazooney what contributed to the deaths of two men, diminished capacity or no diminished capacity, coming over to glad-hand me like he's the official greeter at a gathering of the Hibernian Lodge.

Sada must feel me tensing up because she squeezes my

arm and says under her breath, without moving her lips, "Be good."

"Here comes a big-time pissant," Mabel murmurs on the other side of me.

"You know Bailey?"

"We tangled more than once when I was a detective," he says. "I had to step on him."

"He know you had an operation?" I asks.

Before Mabel can answer, Bailey's in front of me sticking out his hand.

This time I shake it, but not for long.

"They delegated me to intercept you," Bailey says. "This ain't where the ceremony's going to take place. This is just the spillover, all the people wanting to wish us well."

"Us?" I says, picking right up on it.

He grins like a kid with a secret and says, "I meant you, Jimmy. So many people wanting to wish you well, Jim Buckey says rent the whole tavern. Close Schaller's Pump down for the day. The regulars are practically all here anyway. The Central Committee picks up the tab if the Eleventh Ward headquarters can't handle it. The select people is all downstairs."

"Select?" Halstead says.

"You know what I mean," Bailey says, tossing Mabel a look of appreciation. Bailey's an inch or two taller than Halstead which makes her a special attraction, there not being that many big beautiful women around.

"I don't think I been introduced to these charming ladies," Bailey goes on.

"This is my wife's aunt, Sada Spissleman," I says. Bailey practically bows as he takes Aunt Sada's hand.

For a second there I think he's going to lay a kiss on it.

"And this is Mabel Halstead," I says.

Bailey grabs her hand like he don't plan on letting go any-time soon, and grins his best grin into her face.

"Charmed, I'm sure," he says.

I'm wondering what Cary Grant picture he's seen on the late, late show when Mabel says, "Are you?" in the voice which is a little deeper than the voice she usually cultivates.

Bailey, still holding on to Mabel's hand, squints a little and cocks his head like an old dog remembering its lost master's voice even though he seems to be in disguise. Then it dawns on him and he lets go like Mabel's hand was suddenly a red-hot poker.

"Jesus Christ," he says, "I heard something about it but I never . . ." He stops short like his throat's been cut.

"Cat got your tongue, Buck?" Mabel says.

Bailey turns the color of a tomato with splotches. He turns on his heel and walks away fast.

"I don't think we've made a friend there," Aunt Sada says.

"I don't think there was ever a chance of that," Mabel says. "Shouldn't we go downstairs and join the select elite?"

We trot downstairs and out the door, turn left and enter the tavern through the front door, there being no staircase inside the building connecting the two. I think that's because once upon a time the upstairs floor was a separate flat and whoever was living in it, the owner or manager, wanted some privacy. Didn't want drunks wandering upstairs where the wife and kiddies were sleeping.

The noise could stun a mule, a couple of hundred political types all talking at the same time.

Pat Connell, Buck Bailey's sidekick, stationed at the door, spots us and lets out a yell, which rises above the din like the scream of a banshee.

Everybody shuts up and turns to see what triggered it, just in time to see Connell throw his arm around my shoulder like we're the oldest of old buddies, neatly separating me from Aunt Sada and Mabel like he's got a claim on me.

He sticks his mouth close enough to my ear to kiss me on the cheek and says, "Still running with the queers, ain't you, Flannery? What's it do, stick its tongue in your ear?"

I've got no time to go back at him because people are crowding around me from everywhere. Before I know it I'm up at the number one table, Jim Buckey on one side of me and Johnny O'Meara on the other.

Janet Canarias is sitting on the other side of O'Meara and Buck Bailey on the other side of Buckey.

I'm wondering what the bone-breaker's doing up there at the table of honor, but people are crowding up to shake my hand and wish me well, and I got to attend to them. Dozens of them.

I can't name them all who's there, it would take me an hour. Suffice it to say that anybody who was anybody in the Eleventh and in the Twenty-seventh, plus City Hall types and assorted friends and relatives, are all crammed into Schaller's Pump for a grand celebration.

O'Meara stands up and using the bottom of a beer bottle for a gavel gets everybody's attention.

Before they all start gabbing again he says, "Have you all got a sandwich in one hand and a drink in the other?"

A shout goes up.

"Okay, okay, okay. Then we'd better get to doing what we all come here to do or we'll be here until next Christmas. For those of you who don't know me . . ."

He has to wait, standing there grinning as a couple hundred voices make a joke about who doesn't know him.

"Okay, okay, okay," he says again. "Thank you for them kind words. I guess some of you know that I been the committeeman of the Eleventh Ward since I was just a lad."

"I hope you ain't going to start this story when you was in kindergarten," somebody yells out, getting a big laugh.

O'Meara grins good-naturedly and waves a hand for silence. "Okay, okay, okay. I'll make it quick. I been at the job for twenty-eight years and I've been sitting on the city council for more than twelve. So my wife says to me the other day, 'Johnny,' she says, 'don't you think you ought to slow down a little bit?'"

"You try to slow down, you'll fall on your face," the same fan yells out.

"'Give up at least one of your duties,' she says. So you know how it is when your wife makes a suggestion, don't you? Therefore I'm here to announce my retirement as committeeman in the Eleventh."

There's a lot of the usual cheers and boos, demonstrating various feelings of disappointment, regret, joy, and whatever.

"But that don't mean I'm abandoning you. I'll still be in my councilman's office, the usual hours. And I'll be in daily contact with the person what's going to take my place until the next election."

More noise. People at these parties holler whenever anybody finishes a sentence and leaves a blank for them to fill in. If the speaker says their dog's just died, they'd cheer and yell.

"Now I want to introduce to you the man everybody knows, the director of the Democratic Party Central Committee," he goes on, "I give you Mr. Jim Buckey."

The place goes wild again and Buckey stands up, white-haired, slick as a pony in his three-thousand-dollar suit, to take his bows. Here's a man who could've run for public office and won anytime he was of a mind. But he prefers to be the kingmaker, the man behind a thousand thrones.

"What I see here," he says, taking his time scanning the faces in the crowd, "is a lot of old friends from different wards who maybe haven't seen one another for months, maybe years."

Bailey leans forward across the table and turns his head to look at me as though Buckey's talking about us particularly.

"It seems our lives just get busier and busier," Buckey goes on, "until we haven't got time anymore to walk around on a fine spring evening, stopping at this stoop and that porch to chew the fat with this one and that one in our own neighborhoods, let alone in anybody else's neighborhood. And that's really too bad. Thank God for christenings and weddings when old friends get to meet again."

"Don't forget the wakes," somebody shouts.

"I'm not forgetting those," he says, picking it right up, a look on his face halfway between wistful remembering and bittersweet sorrow. "I'm surely not forgetting those. But we're here tonight about the business of the living. There's one among us that at least half of you know, though I'm betting if we counted, it would be nearly all. This is a man who *does* take the time to walk his neighborhoods and plenty of other neighborhoods as well."

"He surely does that," says the character in the crowd.

"Then you know the man I'm talking about. It's my great pleasure, by the authority conferred upon me by my office as director of the State Democratic Party Central Committee, to appoint our own Jimmy Flannery to fill out the term of office, as committeeman of the Eleventh, just relinquished by John O'Meara."

The noise level goes up to what the kids call supersonic.

I get up like a prizefighter just handed the diamond belt, Buckey grabbing me by one wrist and O'Meara by the other, raising my arms above my head.

The crowd surges like they're going to swamp me but Buckey drops my wrist and holds his palms out at the end of stiff arms like he's holding back the flood.

"Hold it! Hold it!" he shouts.

"Okay, okay, okay!" O'Meara yells, dropping my other wrist.

The crowd backs off and gets a little quieter.

"I've got one more announcement to make," Buckey says. "Now that Jimmy Flannery is the committeeman for the Eleventh, it leaves his position open in the Twenty-seventh. I'm happy to announce that a man well known to all of you, many years a precinct captain and loyal party worker, the Twenty-seventh's own Buck Bailey, will finish out Flannery's term of office until the next election."

The place breaks out in another uproar.

I look around to see if I can spot Janet Canarias. She's standing there making a rueful face and when she sees I'm looking at her, she shrugs her shoulders as though to say you got to take the bitter with the better, then holds up a hand, telling me we'll talk later.

Shaftoe's standing next to her and Mabel's standing next to Shaftoe and—you could knock me down with a feather—Joseph Asbach, applauding like crazy, is standing next to Mabel, grinning at her and chatting her up.

Then he turns his head and we're looking at one another, him and me, and his look seems to say, "You came to look me over in my territory, now I'm coming to look you over in yours."

Next thing I know, Bailey's standing next to me, his arm around me like we was the best of friends and the strobe lights are going off.

They're coming by, this long line of well-wishers, shaking my hand and wishing me luck. I get a funny feeling. An insight. Whatever you want to call it.

I realize that I never felt like I was really in politics before. I mean not the way it's written up in the papers and talked about on TV, with all the wheeling and dealing, the mud-slinging and damning with faint praise, the fund-raising and glad-handing. I just thought of myself as a person who liked to help people. I was never two-faced. I never smiled and swallowed anything I couldn't swallow.

Now I knew I was in politics, well and truly. It was a monster that had to be wrestled with, this business of looking at the big picture and the good of all. It was something to be watched or it could eat me up and spit me out, still alive but not the Jimmy Flannery that I used to be.

The next time I looked over at Mabel she's gone and Asbach's gone, too.

I ain't got time to worry about did they leave the party together.

Sixteen

I stay up later than I'm used to doing, eating more potato chips and pickles, and drinking more ginger ale than I should've.

I talk to so many different people that, for once in my life, I can't remember who I talk with.

I know my father took Aunt Sada home pretty early, though I could tell she was ready to hang on until the end.

Buckey and a lot of the other dignitaries are long gone.

At midnight, the party starts to break up, except for a bunch that goes upstairs to the hall on the second floor.

O'Meara's there, a little boozy and teary, moaning and groaning about he's getting old and over the hill, nothing but an old horse put out to pasture. He's getting the sympathy of all his old cronies and some new friends, too, because he's setting them up with boilermakers which ain't on the open bar menu.

I excuse myself and leave the place alone, the Pump an oasis of light and noise in the middle of the quiet night.

I know I should be going home myself but I go over to the storefront in the Twenty-seventh instead.

I use my key and go inside.

There's a light on in Canarias's office. I go over and listen. A radio's playing. I don't know if Janet's in there with someone. Maybe someone she met at Schaller's Pump. Finally I rap very gently on the door.

"Come in, Jimmy," Janet says.

She's sitting behind her desk.

"You didn't have to knock," she says. "I've been waiting for you."

"How did you know I'd be coming here?"

"It's midnight. The party's over. You're all pumped up. You wouldn't know an after-hours club if you fell on one. You want to talk with somebody but your father's home in bed. Mary would get up but she'd probably be able to listen to only half of what you have to say. I had an idea you'd want to chew the fat with someone."

"This is very good of you," I says, setting myself down.

"You did it for me many a time. So, tell me your problem," she says, then grins at me, knowing she's just said what I've said a thousand times a year for a good many years.

"I never been in the service," I says, trying to find a place to start. "But I hear the ex-servicemen talking about being an officer and being in the ranks."

"There're different kinds of responsibilities and privileges," she says. "The enlisted men and women may do all the work and the NCOs may run the outfits, but the officers have to sign for the supplies, give the orders and pay the troops. But most of all they have to take the flak when things go wrong. It may not seem like much, but it's a lot. If you've got a sergeant who gets caught stealing, then the officer in charge is called a thief as well. If there's a soldier puts his hands on an unwilling woman under his orders, then the officer is called a sexual predator too. Old Harry Truman said it best with that sign on his desk. 'The buck stops here.' He understood you couldn't point the finger when every finger's pointed at you."

"So what are you expected to do, times like that, fall on your sword?"

"Sometimes, if things are bad enough, you may be called on to resign, but quitting's easy. What's hard is hiking up your trousers, brushing off your lapels and going out there to give orders again, wondering if you can make them stick."

"I'm not sure I want it," I says. "I'm happy in the ranks. I always told myself I didn't want higher office because it'd keep me from the people, my friends and neighbors, but maybe I was just afraid of climbing the ladder."

"Ladders are funny things, Jimmy, you climb them one rung at a time. You can go down the same way anytime you have a mind to do it."

"But that's not really true, is it?" I says. "You start climbing up there, everybody watching, everybody cheering you on, a lot of them pinning their hopes on you, it's very hard to turn around and go back down because you don't like the view up there."

"So, you hang on, sometimes against your better judgment, and sometimes you crash down all at once, ending up a heap at the bottom," she says.

"Oh, dear," I hear myself say.

"If you've got powerful doubts, Jimmy, now's the time to call a halt. Another step or two and you'll be committed to the journey and then you'll have to take things as they come."

"Oh, dear," I says, surprising myself for showing my agitation out loud. "If you had it to do again, would you do it?" I asks.

"That's too heavy a question for me to lift tonight, Jimmy."

"You talk to Mabel at the party?" I asks.

"We passed the time."

"You see that guy who was chatting her up?"

"Asbach?"

"You know him?"

"No, first time I ever saw him. He introduced himself to me and Mabel. After a couple of minutes he forgot about me. He's a handsome sonofabitch. Devilish-looking, if you know what I mean."

"No, I don't. I don't know what women think is good-looking and what isn't. I think he looks like a snake."

"You know the man?" she asks.

"We had a difference of opinion once upon a time."

"You want to tell me?"

So I tell her about the bombing of the abortion clinic and how, after all these years, Asbach surfaces again on a school council banning books.

We hear somebody open the front door. We hear footsteps crossing the linoleum.

We're both looking at the office door, wondering who it could be, that hour of the morning, when whoever it is raps on the panel.

"Come in," we both say at the same time.

It opens up and Mabel sneaks her head around the door.

"Come in, come in," we both say at the same time again.

She steps through the door looking like she's just stepped

out of a shower and I wonder, like I wondered more than once or twice before, how somebody who looked like a rugged, tough and powerful man not that long ago could look like a big beautiful woman without hardly a trace of masculinity—except maybe her walk every now and then—standing there before us in a short skirt and a blouse that shows off a great set of balconies.

She sits down, sprawls out them long legs and kicks off her shoes.

"I figured you'd be here," she says.

"How'd you figure that?" I asks.

"Sea change. Everybody stays up all night when they have a sea change," Mabel says.

"What's this sea change you're talking about?"

"Things are never going to be the same, Jimmy," Mabel says. "It doesn't look like much now, maybe, but you're the new crown prince. You're being groomed for the throne."

"I've been trying to tell him the same thing," Janet says.

"You disappeared," I says.

"I met someone."

"Someone you know?"

"No, but someone who was tall, dark and good-looking. Shallow me."

"Joe Asbach," Janet says.

Mabel nods and smiles.

"What does he do?" I asks, being casual about it.

"He's in insurance."

"What kind of insurance would that be?"

"Medical," Mabel says, like that's the end of the interrogation.

Janet and me sit there, not knowing what else to say. If Mabel don't want to tell us anything about what happened between her and this guy Asbach until nearly two o'clock in the morning, what else can we do but sit there grinning at each other like a bunch of idiots, feeling good in each other's company?

Seventeen

I'm wondering how come Maggie Lundatos wasn't at the celebration over to Schaller's Pump when I was named warlord of the Eleventh.

I didn't have to wonder long. Three days later I get a call at my office in Janet's storefront which I ain't quite moved out of yet.

"Hello, Jimmy, this is Maggie."

"I missed you at the appointment celebration," I says.

"Did you? Well, I thought it best staying out of the public eye. But that doesn't mean I want to be left out of the loop. Would you mind meeting with me to discuss some strategy?"

I hesitate for a couple of seconds.

It's a funny kind of thing. If there was no doubt in my mind that we'd be nothing but political associates then I wouldn't hesitate for one minute meeting her anywhere and anytime there seemed to be reason for a meeting. After all I meet with attractive women all the time. So it's my feelings that make me afraid that other people would become suspicious if they see us together too much.

It's like going to a party and seeing two people who've been friends and who've become, unbeknownst to others, something a lot more. Where before they'd touch the other to get his or her attention, or to hold his or her attention while they make a conversational point, now they avoid touching so carefully that right away you know that something's up.

"When would you like to get together?" I asks.

"Like Rudy Vallee used to sing, 'My time is your time,' " she says, some laughter in her voice the way women's voices get when they know they're confusing some poor male.

"Rudy Vallee?" I says.

"I guess you're not a fan of old motion pictures. I'm simply saying that I can easily fit my schedule to suit your pleasure."

So now I'm wondering is it just me who hears double meanings in everything she says.

"Jimmy?" she says, emphasizing the fact that I'm still hanging in there without saying anything.

"How about this afternoon?" I asks.

Now it's her turn to hesitate.

"Not good?" I asks.

"I was just thinking about having to do my hair and getting dressed to go out on such short notice. I'm in my grubbies doing some repairs around the house."

"Doing what?" I says, hardly able to imagine Maggie with a feather duster in her hands, let alone a wrench.

"Oh, I'm pretty handy. I've got a clogged drain in the sink. It's easier for me to fix it than schedule a plumber. You mind coming over here?" she asks, as though the thought just that second came into her head.

I get the feeling again that I'm a fly about to put a foot on a spider's web but I figure I'm a big boy now and should certainly be able to handle myself if a situation should come up.

"All right. It's ten o'clock. When?"

"Thirty minutes? Do you know where I live?"

"I'll need an address," I says.

She gives me the address of a condominium tower on the Gold Coast over to the Near North Side, one of the most interesting parts of the city because it's probably the most diverse. It roughly follows the outline of the Forty-second Ward where an acquaintance of mine, George Dunne, is alderman.

It's got the Miracle Mile along Michigan Avenue where a person can buy just about anything you can think of from just about anyplace in the world, Rush Street where the nightlife concentrates, Streeterville and Sandburg Village, between Division Street and North Avenue, a prime example of pushing the poor out of low-cost housing to build luxury flats in a prime location.

I expect Maggie Lundatos to be living along Lake Shore Drive where the really rich and famous live but, instead, she lives over to River Wharf, a condominium tower at State Street and the river, which ain't exactly Cabrini Green but could be called the second layer on the cake.

I drive over, thinking about how I used to take the El practically every chance I got and how now I practically never do, taking my car instead, because I want it standing by so I can get here or there on a moment's notice.

There's a doorman at the front entrance who's been trained not to look down his nose at old vehicles like what I drive.

"Yes, sir?" he says when I lean across the passenger's seat and roll down the window.

"I got an appointment upstairs. Is there anyplace around here where I can park my car?"

"We have visitor's parking underground. The entrance is around the corner."

"Thank you," I says.

"Sir? Will I announce you?"

"I can handle it," I says, and drive around to the garage entrance.

The elevator drops me off in the lobby where another uniformed guard sits at a desk. He looks me over as I approach, then smiles and says, "Go right on up, Mr. Flannery," pointing me to another elevator all by itself in the corner. "Last elevator in a row. The others require a key."

I walk down the carpet with the feeling that he's smirking behind my back. I wonder does Maggie have any male visitors in the morning and I get a hot flash of jealousy.

The car whizzes me up to the top floor and lets me out into a foyer as big as my living room with mirrors at each end, gray carpeting with two flokati rugs under the mirrors. The bust of some Greek god is standing on each of two pillars reflected in the mirrors. I feel like I'm walking into a museum.

The door to the flat is already wide open.

Maggie's amplified voice says, practically at my shoulder, "Down the corridor on your right and follow it into the kitchen."

I leave the carpet and walk down a floor made of black and white squares of marble. Up ahead of me is a doorway with nothing but white behind it, like a quarry in the sun.

The kitchen is nothing but white, white floor, white

countertops, white Corian cabinets and sinks, white furniture. The only color is a bowl of pink roses and a double row of copper frying pans on a clear plastic rod above the cooktop.

I don't see Maggie anywhere.

I'm counting the frying pans above my head when she says, "Hey," from where she's sitting on the floor.

I got to admit that I was half expecting her to meet me at the door in a negligee with a martini in each hand, which goes to show you how even a man who thinks he's trying to avoid temptation can go around with really ridiculous and outrageous fantasies in his head.

Anyway, she ain't wearing a negligee, she's wearing gray sweats. Not even them fancy tights with a kind of abbreviated swimsuit over them which the women wear to show off what they pretend they're trying to hide, but just old army-navy store sweats. Her hair's up in a red bandanna and there's a swipe of grease on her cheek. She's so gorgeous it could stop your heart. So right then and there I know I'm in a lot more trouble than I ever thought I was.

"You doing any good under there?" I asks.

"I got it fixed."

She reaches up her hand, not making any excuses for the grease, and I pull her up to her feet. She sort of bounces on her toes, looking up into my face, which is an experience because I'm not that tall, and she smiles at me for a second. But she don't turn the power on.

"You eat breakfast?" she asks.

"I didn't find the time this morning."

"Eggs? Or are you being careful about your cholesterol?"

"I try to be."

"These are low-cholesterol eggs. Truly. They breed a special kind of chicken and feed them a special diet. Reach me down three of those pans, two small and one medium."

She's lighting three of the burners on the gas top, taking a bowl of eggs and another dish of something . . . I don't know what . . . out of a refrigerator concealed in the wall.

"Polenta," she says. "Do you like polenta?"

"For breakfast?" I says.

"The way I make it. Better than sausage or bacon."

She's slicing and spicing the polenta, picking up the eggs one by one and shaking them a little by her ear, putting a film of oil and a touch of butter in the pans.

"Sunny-side up, over easy, omelet or scrambled?"

"Scrambled."

"Moist or dry?"

"Moist."

"A man after my own heart. Coffee, tea, or milk?"

"Coffee."

"Pick a pot. The one on the right is regular French Roast. The one on the left is Colombian decaf. Both freshly brewed."

"You having coffee, too?" I asks.

"What's good for you is good for me."

"Regular?"

"Suits me."

I pour two cups of coffee at the table. She's breaking eggs in a bowl and whisking them up with a shot of cream.

"You ready for an adventure?" she asks.

"What?"

"Let me surprise you," she says, hesitating in her work and looking at me.

"Okay," I says.

She takes some cream cheese from a keeper, pours half the

egg mixture in one pan and half in the other, adds a table-spoon full of cream cheese in the middle of each pan, and breaks it up with a fork.

"Soft cream cheese," she says. "Low-cal, low-cholesterol. Do you put jelly on your eggs?" she says.

"You do that?" I asks, because I been putting jelly on my eggs ever since I was a kid. Everybody else puts on ketchup or Tabasco but I put on jelly. "What kind you got?"

"What kind you want? Take a look in that fridge right there," she says, pointing with a spatula, never taking her eyes off the eggs.

I open the door. This refrigerator is only one jar deep and every kind of jelly, jam, dressing and sauce is lined up like soldiers.

"Guava for me," she says.

I take down the jar of guava and I'm about to take down some blackberry or apple for myself when I decide to try guava.

By the time I get to the table by the window with the jelly, she's got the eggs and polenta on the plates.

We sit down and start on the eggs. I never tasted anything like them.

"Do you know," she says, "the test of any restaurant chef is an order of scrambled eggs cooked moist."

"Why's that?" I asks, enjoying myself no end.

"They have to be watched constantly. The cook can't take his or her eye off them for a second. The pans have to be taken off the fire at just the right moment because they con-tinue to cook in the time it takes to move them from pan to plate."

She takes another forkful of eggs, cheese and jelly and makes a satisfied sound like a purr.

My heart jumps in my chest.

Over a second cup of coffee we start talking politics.

It's more than just she understands the ins and outs, how to spot the levers of influence and how to use them, when to push and when to lay back. She knows the subtleties, how to read the truth in an eye, hear what's really being said. She talks in such a way that I know her skin tells her things about what's going on in any given situation. That happens to me and I can't tell you what joy there is in it.

I've talked politics with my old man all my life and with operators like Delvin and Dunleavy since I was twenty. Aunt Sada knows more than a thing or two and Janet Canarias is as good as they come.

But the way Maggie Lundatos talks, describing the ins and outs of Washington, I know she's an artist. A poet of politics.

"So, you don't mind my asking, how did you miss advising Leo against what he was doing?" I asks.

"I couldn't make my influence obvious. I couldn't challenge him. He still has old-world macho values. Oh, sure, I had his ear on the pillow but I didn't often sit down in the smoke-filled rooms and when I did all the men got polite. It's like raising a kid. You can do all the right things, give all the right advice, but when they're at school, their peer group is more powerful than any parent can ever be. I couldn't teach him how to stop being a ward politician."

She looks at me fondly. "Not that being a ward politician, a great ward politician, isn't a very good thing indeed."

Two hours and a second pot of coffee go by like that, before I glance at the clock and realize I got places to go and things to do.

You remember that old Jimmy Durante song what goes,

"Did you ever have the feeling that you wanted to go, but then you have the feeling that you wanted to stay? I'll go. I'll stay"? Well, that's exactly how I felt about sitting there in Maggie's kitchen, talking politics with her.

Going down in the elevator I got two other thoughts and feelings.

One. I can't remember the last time when I had such a good time.

Two. When I was thinking about how Maggie was so much better at politics than practically anyone I ever knew, and how talking to her cleared my head about strategies and tactics better than anyone I ever consulted with, even old Delvin, I didn't once compare her to Mary.

She's my life's mate and my heart's love and the keeper of the hearth and the mother of my child but, the truth is, she's got no more than a passing interest in politics and that's only because it's what I do.

I can appreciate how far a man could go in politics with a woman like Maggie alongside him.

After that first time, I go to her flat in the sky almost every time she asks, which is about every other morning for more than a month. We sit at the kitchen table with the view of Chicago and the lake spread out down below, eating eggs with jelly and cream cheese, and sometimes things like French toast, drinking coffee and teaching each other everything we know about politics and getting along with people. I tell myself I'm making plans for my future campaigns but every once in a while I admit to myself that maybe I just want to be with Maggie.

Down at work, my boss calls me in and tells me I should take some free time settling into the office I get in the

Eleventh Ward Democratic Headquarters just across the street from Schaller's Pump. I'm being given special privileges and I ain't complaining.

O'Meara offers to sublet the offices he's had for hisself in a building just around the corner but I tell him I don't want to be taking on any extra expense until I get my feet on the ground and know what I'm going to need.

My new office ain't much bigger than the one I had in Janet's storefront but it's all me and Mabel really need.

Eighteen

I had every intention of going over to Lloyd Moraine's house and see if I could have a talk with him about this book-banning business, but it got away from me. I call his office to see if I can drop by and have a chat but I'm told he's not been to work that day.

So I take the chance and walk over to his house on Sangamon from my house on Aberdeen.

I feel like I used to feel when most of my business and errands was in my own neighborhood instead of scattered all over the place. As I walk along, I'm thinking that maybe the reason I didn't follow up sooner was because I was like the reporters Shaftoe talks about what don't want to do the leg-work. Or maybe I'm ducking it because I ain't resolved in my own mind what's my stand on a book like *Daddy's Roommate*.

Moraine's house is a big, light gray three-story, with dormers in the roof, which looks like it could use a new coat of paint. Looking at the plants and flowers you can tell it ain't being neglected but that he just ain't got around to it.

I climb the steps to the wide porch. There's old wicker

furniture on it which has been freshly painted. I wonder how often he sits out there on a fine spring or summer evening these days, what with television and all.

I don't even get to ring the bell. I'm two steps away from the front door when it opens up and a thin guy, maybe seventy-five, maybe more, opens up and stands there looking me over in a way that ain't at all unfriendly.

"Hello," I says. "My name's Jimmy Flannery and I'm your new Democratic Party committeeman."

"Didn't you stop into my office down at Education about a month ago?" he says.

"Yes, I did."

"That was before you were appointed warlord of the Eleventh?"

"Yes, sir, it was."

"Which means you weren't stopping by just to introduce yourself on that occasion."

"That's right, I wasn't."

"Which means you wanted something."

"Well . . ."

"You still want something?"

"A little conversation," I says.

"Well, why don't we sit right here on the porch and see what we can do. I'd ask you in but my wife's not feeling well."

"I was told she'd had some health problem."

"Surgery. She's getting better but she has days when she doesn't feel up to it. That's why I'm home with her."

"Lloyd? Lloyd? You, Lloyd!" a voice comes from inside the house.

"What is it, Mary?" he shouts over his shoulder.

"Who's that you're talking to out there?"

"You don't know him. Just a neighbor stopped by."

"Try me," she says. "Give me a name."

"Flannery," he says.

"Jimmy Flannery," I says, raising my voice.

"Sure, I know you," she says. "Mike Flannery's boy. Of course I know you. Well, I don't know you but I heard of you. Lloyd, you bring him in here so I can see what he looks like."

"All right, Mary, right after we have a little sit and chat on the porch."

"Well, open the window a little wider so I can hear what's said."

"You should be resting, Mary," he says.

"Do like I ask, Lloyd, or I'll turn you in on a new model."

He smiles at me and goes to open the window in the living room bay a little wider, sticking his head in and saying, "You keep a wrap around your shoulders. All you need is to get a cold."

Then he pulls his head back out and gestures to one of the wicker armchairs and sits down in another.

"My wife's name is Mary," I says. "My mother's name was Mary, too, God rest her soul."

"Don't hear that much anymore," he says.

"The name Mary?"

"No, the blessing. Okay, let's hear it. What did you come to see me about?"

"Book banning," I says, coming right out with it.

"Any book in particular you want banned?"

"I don't want any book banned."

"You're protesting the banning of a book, then?"

"Yes, I guess I am."

"You here representing yourself or one of your constituents?"

"Representing a friend."

"He or she wants to file a protest or complaint about a banned book, it should properly begin at the school council level."

"I thought it might not be a bad idea to get the word on official policy before taking that step."

"Talk to the generals and never mind the field officers, is that right?"

"What do you think?"

"I think . . . no, I know . . . that there is no official policy about the banning of books or the censorship of unacceptable written, audio or visual materials."

"Why is that?"

"Because it's shifting ground. Look, books are banned for any number of reasons, but most often it's either because of ethnic slur or unacceptable content. Which is yours?"

"The second. A couple of books were banned over to Bochos Elementary by the council there."

"Which two?"

"*A Thousand Acres* and *Daddy's Roommate* among the usual suspects."

"Oh, those two. Have you read them?"

"Well, no I haven't."

"You'd better get on the stick, Flannery."

"I haven't had the time . . ."

I let it drift off because he's grinning at me.

"Never mind. I understand. Nobody's got the time anymore. Those two books, it seems as though they're on just about everybody's hit list. So your problem is the local banning of a couple of books which the school council has deemed pornographic?"

"Would you call them pornographic?"

"Doesn't matter what I think. If the Supreme Court left the determination of pornography up to community standards, how do you expect any municipal administrative board to do anything different?"

"So, you can't give me any help on this?"

"Read the books, then you come back and tell me if you want me to interfere with Bochos Elementary School council on this one."

The wicker creaks as Moraine gets up. I get up too.

"You leaving, Mr. Flannery?" Mary says from inside the room, on the other side of the open window with the curtains moving in the breeze.

"Yes, ma'am," I says.

"Well, you come in here first."

We go inside through a hallway much like the one in my house, and into a living room that smells of flowers.

Mary Moraine's lying on a chaise. She's wearing a flowered housecoat and she's got a scarf around her head covering her hair. She looks me over and smiles.

"I like your looks," she says.

I don't know if I blush or not.

"May I call you Jimmy, Mr. Flannery?"

"I wish you would."

"And may I give you a little piece of advice?"

"Sure."

"With that red hair and that cocky grin, I'd watch myself around unattached women."

I know she was making a funny compliment but it also had the ring of prophecy. You got to watch out for Irish grandmothers, they'll worry you to death with feelings of guilt for things you ain't even done yet.

Nineteen

When I get the message from Leo Lundatos that he'd appreciate a visit from me, I ain't altogether surprised. I know enough about people working in service jobs—waiters, doormen, security guards, and so forth—to know that it's only a short distance in their heads between a gratuity and bribe. Besides, at a time when the social contract between industry and labor, management and labor, employer and employee has broken down, when loyalty has been thrown out the window and promises broken, there's very few people who feel an obligation to protect the privacy of them what's paying their wages.

It could've been the doorman at Maggie's building or the security guard who waves me toward the private elevator with this knowing little smirk on his mouth who gives Lundatos the tip. They could even be on Leo's payroll for a double sawbuck each time they come up with a bit of news he might find useful.

Or it might be somebody in my own organization. Somebody new like Shaftoe, or somebody old like Mabel.

So here I am getting paranoid.

But the point is, Lundatos may have reached out to me and give me his blessing in spite of the pressure I put on him to get out of public life before he got sent to the Club Fed. Then again he might be playing a game on me, keeping me sweet in case he wants to use me in the future.

I find it a little hard to believe that he's standing still for this divorce coming his way. He could very well still consider Maggie his property, no matter what she might think. He might've already made up his mind he ain't going to make it easy for her.

So here I am driving up to Duluth, Minnesota, to the federal prison camp there, one of them prisons without fences, where convicted official wrongdoers take their ease in five- or six-man cottages, complete with kitchens and a television room, swimming in the pool, doing a little gardening, getting in a couple sets of tennis and working on their tans.

It's as easy to walk into the facility as it would be to walk out of it. Everything's very casual, very polite, like the guards figure, who knows, there could come a time when one of these very important people they're watching over could do them a favor. The individuals sentenced to a stay in this place may be temporarily in disgrace, but everybody knows all they got to do after they get out is make a couple of phone calls and they'll be back in the loop. It'll be like they was off for a long holiday in the Bahamas.

They'll go on the lecture circuit, confessing their sins and giving the audience hints about how to avoid the potholes they stepped in.

Leo's in front of the cottage on his knees working on a flower bed. He's wearing garden gloves and when he stands up I can see he's wearing knee pads, he shouldn't get his pressed denims dirty.

He takes off his glove and sticks out his hand. "How's it shakin', Flannery?" he says.

The man looks five years younger and ten years fitter than he did the last time I see him. He's got a tan which makes his white hair look whiter. His smile could blind you.

"Come on inside. I can't offer you anything but tea, hot or cold, or a cup of coffee."

"Nothing, thanks," I says, following him inside.

"We'll talk in my room where we won't be disturbed," he says.

It's a nice room. Nothing fancy. More like a room at a boys' camp or the NCO quarters in an army barracks, except Lundatos don't have to share with anybody.

"Sit down. Sit down," he says, offering me the chair placed alongside a reading lamp.

The brilliant smile's never left his face and I know that ain't a good sign with sharks or baboons.

I sit in the chair. He sits on the bed.

"How's your organization shaping up?" he asks.

"Pretty good," I says. "It's more like volunteer staff at the moment. No need to gear up for the campaign for alderman until the beginning of next year, the end of this."

"You start down the road to higher office, Jimmy, you don't have to worry about when to start campaigning because you never stop campaigning."

"Well, yes, I can understand what you're saying," I says.

"So, okay then, who've you got servicing the committeeman's office that you can switch over to the campaign?"

"Well, I have a woman by the name of Mabel Halstead

managing the office. Also you could say she's my number one aide."

"Interesting person you got there. Ex-cop, right?"

"That's right."

"Ex-man, right?"

"Mabel had some gender difficulty but she straightened it out."

"Who else you got?"

"My wife's aunt, Sada Spissleman's, going to run my campaign."

"Mo Spice's widow?"

"Yes."

"Socialist."

I don't say anything.

"Who you got for a bird dog?"

"Bird dog?" I says.

"Run your errands. Sniff things out?"

"Sniff out what?"

"Where the opposition keeps the rotten meat. Who's got sticky fingers and stinky feet."

"I don't think I need anybody like that. If there's things I need looked into, I got a man by the name of Willy Dink."

"That's good. Used to be an exterminator, right?"

"Well, he used to take care of cockroaches and rats and things like that."

"Which is what I'm saying."

I got an idea that Lundatos is thinking about a different kind of extermination than cockroaches and mice, but I don't say anything because Willy Dink seems to be the only person on what you might call my staff that Lundatos approves of so far, in spite of the fact that Dink was the one who gives me the evidence with which I apply the squeeze to Lundatos.

"Who else you got?" he asks.

"My father's ready to knock on doors."

"Even at his age? Isn't that wonderful? Your father'll be a big asset. The older people get out there and vote. With your old man out there in front, you can put the over-sixty vote in your pocket. Who for strategy?"

"Janet Canarias, the alderman from the Twenty-seventh."

"Dyke."

"A very good friend."

"So, that's all right, she'll help you get the deviants."

I'm ready to walk out of there but I learned long ago that walking away from ignorant bigots don't do anybody any good. Neither does arguing with them. You change the minds of bigots by putting them in a position where they want something so much that they'll sit down with the people they hate and maybe find out they're all human beings after all.

"Anybody else important to your campaign? Never mind the soldiers or the field officers, so to speak," he says, "just give me the general staff."

"That does it, I think," I says.

A look flashes in his eye like a cat what just caught a mouse, or a frog what just caught a fly. Like he's caught me out in a lie.

"Well, how about little Bobby Shaftoe?"

I deliberately don't mention Shaftoe just to see how long it'll be before Lundatos brings him up. So he knows about Shaftoe, calls him Bobby. Could mean he knows him very well or could be he's just sort of sneering at the man.

"Well, now, how about my dear wife?" he goes on. "How about Maggie? You forget all about her?"

"Well, no, I didn't forget about her."

"Just slipped your mind, all these times you've been up to her condominium enjoying the view, maybe having a little breakfast?"

"Maggie's not on my staff. She's a friend."

"And a heavy contributor to your campaign?"

"I sent her generous contribution back," I says.

"No use for it yet? Of course not. But she'll be there with wallet or purse when you're really ready to roll, right?"

"My policy about the size and source of contributions is down on paper. It's the same for one and all."

"So, it's just socializing, you being in my wife's apartment day after day?"

"I'm learning what she can teach me," I says.

He smiles a smile that calls me a liar and a womanizer and a wife stealer and God knows what else. He's got me on the run all because I didn't come right out with it and tell him I'd been seeing his soon-to-be ex-wife before he could bring it up.

"I'll just bet," he says. He's playing the outraged husband, helpless and impotent through circumstance, who has to sit by and watch his happy marriage destroyed by an opportunist and a thief. It's partly an act but it's partly what he believes because he wants to believe it.

It was my mistake, not being up-front about her. Was it because in my heart of hearts I knew going over there, seeing her so much, was not out of the best of motives? Was I like a kid playing with fire and afraid to admit it?

"I got to assure you there's nothing going on here," I says, hating the way it sounds, like I'm covering up a guilty secret.

"Look at the situation from where I'm sitting," Lundatos says.

I feel like saying that where he's sitting is in a tub of butter.

"It's not a week after I walk into this joint that my wife of many years informs me that she's filing for divorce," he goes on.

"Wouldn't you say that she finally got fed up with you fooling around with professional ladies and . . ."

"Are you crazy? We had an understanding. She's in Washington with me and I'm a good husband. But I got to spend my time here in the city, making myself available to the voters and I'm alone and lonely. There's a lot of separation. She understands I'm a man of strong appetites."

I feel like telling him did he ever think that she's a woman of strong appetites, too, and just how far did the understanding go?

"She don't necessarily condone but she accepts the fact that I need occasional relief," he says.

Which you take wherever and whenever with whoever, I think to myself.

"But then you come along, Flannery."

I don't mention that he dragged me into his circle; I didn't elbow my way in. He thought he could use me, so he threw his wife in my face, figuring I was also a man of strong appetites and easy conscience like hisself. She was a temptation.

I hear myself thinking the way I'm thinking and all of a sudden I don't like it. So I stand up.

"Where do you think you're going?" Lundatos says.

"I don't like where this conversation's going," I says. "The next thing, you'll be accusing me of stealing your wife away from you. I met the lady two or three times before you put your foot into it up to your neck."

"There you are," he shouts, jumping up from the bed. "You just proved my point. I never said you were a dumbbell. You see her maybe twice all them weeks and since I walked through the gates here you've seen her a dozen times that many."

"Okay, I'll give you that. It looks a little funny from the outside looking in."

"From the inside looking out," he sticks in there.

"So would you like it better if Maggie and me met in public places?"

"I'd like it better you didn't meet with her at all," he says in this very flat, very quiet way which is a lot more threatening than shouting.

"I don't know if you got a say in it anymore. Maggie don't consider she owes you anything anymore."

"Oh, I still got something to say about it. You just go on fooling around my wife and you'll find out I still got a say. And you'll find out that actions speak louder than words."

"I don't know was that a threat, Mr. Lundatos, or if your feelings just got the better of you, but I got to tell you that I don't take easy to threats. I told you that there was nothing between me and your wife, and I don't intend there ever will be, but I'm going to see her anytime she wants to see me, because she's a friend, and I got no guilty feelings."

Twenty

Joe Medill, the columnist for the *Tribune*, wants to do a profile on me for the Sunday Magazine section.

I asks him will that put Jackie Boyle's nose out of joint, him being a longtime friend of mine just like Joe.

"So, let him do one on you, too, if he wants to," Medill says. "It ain't like we're doing a scoop here, Flannery. Whatever you got to say ain't going to shake the body politic."

Which in its own way is not a very complimentary remark.

We set a date and time to meet over to Schaller's Pump.

I call Boyle to see if that's all right with him.

"Sure, that's all right with me," Boyle says. "I'll meet you over to Schaller's, but what's the meeting all about?"

"Joe Medill wants to do a profile on me and I didn't want you to think I was giving him an exclusive over you."

"A profile, is it?" Boyle says. "Well, that is grand, but I don't think I want to do any more than a column . . . maybe a mention. I mean, after all, Flannery, anything you have to say ain't going to make headlines."

So here I am getting interviewed by two columnists who don't think much of who they're going to write about.

I get to Schaller's about eight o'clock. There's quite a crowd sitting at the tables and bellied up to the bar. I tuck myself between Medill and Boyle, what already got their paws wrapped around a couple of pints which I, no doubt, will be expected to pay for. I order a ginger ale from Harry Fannon, the bartender.

He sets me up and I'm about to take a swallow when somebody taps me on the shoulder with a stiff finger. It's very funny how you can tell when a finger ain't friendly, so I look over my shoulder expecting to see trouble.

Bailey's standing there with his buddy Connell right behind his shoulder.

"When are you going to start drinking a real drink . . . a man's drink . . . Flannery?"

"When are you going to sit down and mind your own business, Bailey?" I asks. "But, since it's on your mind, let me tell you that ginger ale was the drink of Irish kings before Guinness stout was invented."

"And you're an Irish sonofabitch who'd lie to his own priest."

"How'd we bring the Church into this?" I says. "If I were you, Bailey, I'd be the one to switch drinks. You better put that whiskey aside and have a ginger ale with me."

"You can shove your ginger ale up your ass, Flannery."

"Why are you pushing for a fight, Bailey? I can see you got an early start on tonight's drunk and tomorrow's hangover, but why are you acting so foolish?"

"That bitch won't let me share her office the way she lets you share her office."

"If you're talking about Janet Canarias, then I guess all I

got to say is that she's got a right to have who she wants sharing the storefront. Go rent your own office."

"I already have."

"Then, if you got time on your hands, why ain't you in it learning your ward and your job?"

"For one thing Canarias ain't making it any easier for me. She ain't giving me a hell of a lot of cooperation dealing with citizen requests and complaints I bring to her."

"I'm sure anything she feels needs doing by her gets done or at least looked into. The idea is that you're supposed to take some of the burden off her. You're the filter between the people and the government."

"I'm no fucking filter. I'm the warlord of the Twenty-seventh," he sputters in my face.

"You're an asshole spitting on me," I says, "and if you don't back off pretty damn quick I'm going to poke a straw up your nose."

"Why you little fuck," he says, getting even closer, "I'll chew you up like you was a cherry and spit you out like you was the pit."

"I don't know how you're going to do that without your teeth," I says, putting the flat of my hand on his chest and backing him off.

Then I start to laugh. Don't ask me why but I start to laugh. It ain't a nervous laugh because I'm afraid I'm about to be in a fight. I'm laughing because here we are making threats to one another like a couple of kids in the playground. Me laughing gets Medill and Boyle to laughing.

It's the wrong thing to do. Bailey turns red and hauls off to give me a fist in the face, which is a stupid thing bullies do, this big windup like they mean to knock your head off. While his hambone of a fist is still back there over his shoulder ready to be fired, I smack him twice in the face, forehand, backhand, one two.

While he's recovering from the surprise of that, I grab his lapels and bring his head down to the height of my head and crack the bone in his nose.

He lets out a hell of a yell as I shove him back, he shouldn't bleed on me, and he goes down on his ass, hollering like a wounded bull.

Connell almost goes down with him, but steps aside just in time and keeps his feet.

Now Connell's coming at me, cocking his fist just like Bailey done.

"Hey, idiot," I says, "you just see what happened to your pal? Well, think about it. It could happen to you."

He thinks about it.

"Pick up your buddy," I says.

He bends down and gets Bailey under the armpits.

"You didn't even catch me, for Christ's sake," Bailey says to Connell. "You let me slip and fall on my ass."

"You didn't exactly slip and fall," Connell says. "More like Flannery knocked you on your ass."

"That little fart knocked me on my ass? What the hell are you talking about?" Bailey says.

"Hey, Mr. Flannery," Harry Fannon says, "you mind taking a walk until I get this straightened out? Half an hour?"

Some people would take offense as the innocent party but I know that Fannon's working it the right way, always get the reasonable combatant out of the way so you can cool the drunk down.

"Come on across the street to my office," I says to Medill and Boyle. "I got a pint of rye for my guests in the desk drawer."

Medill gets a double handful of ginger ale splits from Fannon and we leave Schaller's Pump and go to my office where we pour some drinks and talk about my political career, such as it is, with special emphasis on the number of times I been involved in cases of murder and mayhem through no fault of my own.

Twenty-one

Medill and Boyle leave when the pint's finished.

The fight, such as it was, has still got me all pumped. If I go home, I'm going to toss and turn and wake Mary up.

So I decide to go over to Janet's office in the Twenty-seventh and clean up any ward business I still got on my desk.

I find Mabel sitting in my chair with her long legs stretched out and her feet up on the desk.

"You still running around this time of night?" she says.

"Well, I ain't doing more than you're doing," I says, taking the visitor's chair on the other side of the desk. "You shouldn't be here this late."

"I had a few things I wanted to clean up."

"You can't give all your time to this job," I says. "You got to have a social life."

"Oh, I've got a social life," she says. "I just came from enjoying some of my social life."

The way she puts the emphasis on this word and that I can hear the hurt and bitterness pouring out. Then I can see she's been crying.

"I can see you're very upset, you don't mind my noticing," I says. "You want to talk to me about anything?"

She looks right into my eyes for a long minute like she's studying me for signs of sympathy or pity.

She's trying to read me and I'm trying to read her. I don't know if either of us is getting very far.

"Can you use a little help clearing up whatever it is troubling you?" I says, coaxing her a little bit.

"What do you think of me, Jimmy?" she asks.

"I think you're one of the nicest, bravest people I ever met."

"Don't get all sweet and silly on me. The next thing you'll be telling me is that you find me an interesting individual."

"Well, I do."

"Okay, that's a given. What's not interesting about a six-foot broad with a thirty-six C cup? But you knew me before and you know me after. Milton and Mabel, the Siamese twins, joined at the hip. You must have mixed feelings when you see me with my legs up on the desk showing half an acre of thigh."

She puts her feet on the floor as though taking temptation out of my sight.

"You know, sometimes, I still find myself sitting or standing or moving the way I did when I was a man." She leans forward. "Isn't it confusing to contemplate the essential me and the physical me?"

"From what you told me about the soul-searching you had to go through before you decided to have the operation, it seems to me the physical you and the essential you and the sexual and even the spiritual you come as a package. Maybe because you had to, like, first find yourself and then invent yourself, you seem a lot more whole than a lot of people I know."

"It's sweet of you to say all that, Jimmy, but the fact is I've never felt whole in my entire life. Not before the operation and certainly not afterward. I appreciate what I got by going through with it but I also know what I lost."

"I can understand," I says.

Her mouth twists up in a little smile, like she wants to say, "Well, no, you don't," but is too polite to brush me off that way.

"The only time I can feel really easy," she says, "is when I'm with people like Janet, who's got her own demons to wrestle with, and people like you, who knew me before and after. People I don't have to hide anything from. At least not too much."

She starts to tear up and turns her head away, like a man not wanting a friend to see him cry or a woman afraid she'll be considered weak.

"It's very hard to know how much truth new friends can take," she says. "If I think someone can handle it and I guess wrong, then I can lose the friendship—"

"Maybe that person wouldn't've made much of a friend in the first place," I says.

"—and sometimes a lot more than that," she goes on as though she didn't even hear me.

"If you got doubts about somebody, then I guess all you can do is keep the truth to yourself," I says.

"Then I feel like a liar and a fraud."

She looks away again and I know she's trying to hide the look in her eyes the way people do when they're remembering something that hurts.

"Did you tell someone the truth tonight?" I asks.

She looks at me again and shakes her head in admiration. "Ah, Jimmy, Jimmy," she says with the hint of an Irish brogue, "you've got an eye as sharp as a raven's and a heart as soft as a bun. That's exactly what happened. We were in a place . . . a situation . . . a very intimate situation . . . and I felt safe and secure and . . . loved . . . and I . . ."

She stands up all of a sudden, whatever comes next obviously too painful for her to go on, and says, "Are we ready to get the hell out of here?"

I get up and go get her jacket off the hook. I help her on with it, treating her like she's somebody small and delicate. I turn out all the lights. I pull down the green shade which covers the glass pane in the front door. I set the alarm. We walk out and I lock the door.

There's nothing and nobody on the street. It's so quiet it's hard to believe, for a second there, that we're in the middle of a big city. Then a car starts on a side street and breaks the silence. A pair of headlights flare and the car comes out onto the main street, picking up speed as it straightens out from the turn.

Mabel's grabbing me and turning me around toward the doorway. "Get down," she yells, crouching lower behind me, shielding my body with her own as she crowds me into the doorway, the only shelter available to us. I hear three shots like the clapping of hands. Her whole weight crushes me into the door and through the glass. The alarm goes off.

I'm laying there on the floor inside the storefront with Mabel sprawled on top of me. I get out from under. I make it to my feet and stand there shaking.

"What the hell was that all about?" I says. "You all right?"

She don't say anything back to me. She just lays there.

Some light from a nearby streetlamp spills through the broken door. There's blood all over the back of her blouse.

When the cops arrive I'm on my knees beside her (they later tell me), begging her to get up and calling her Milton.

These cops is a team I know, Chalky Butts and Penny Tucker. Tucker's the one helps me to my feet and into my office while Butts calls in the homicide and the location.

It seems to me Tucker's hardly finished asking me do I want a glass of water when O'Shea and Rourke, these old detective friends of mine, are there.

I think I once described O'Shea as a man with a face like a raw side of beef and a kidney for a nose. Right from the minute I first meet him I figure him for the meanest cop I'm ever going to come up against. He works hard to prove me right.

But the years have passed and though his temper ain't got much sweeter he's revealed a liking for me which may be grudging but appears to be genuine. Also his hair's turning white and he's lost some of the color in his face, but the nose still looks like a kidney.

Rourke's the sweetheart of the two, the one who plays good cop and gets criminals to confide in him. But I've seen him when he's turned as cold as ice and you know that a killer sleeps behind his eyes.

"You all right, Flannery?" O'Shea asks.

"I ain't been shot but I ain't all right, either," I says.

"Is that Milton Halstead in there?" he asks.

"Mabel. How did you know she was Milton?"

"ID in her purse. She still carries her cop's card."

"You know her?" I asks.

"I knew her when he was a cop."

"He was a good cop," Rourke says.

"She was a good person," I says.

"You up for telling us what happened?" Rourke says.

"I stopped over here to the office to tie up some loose ends."

"Loose ends you had to tie up this hour of the night?"

"Sometimes the day gets longer than I'd like and sometimes a week gets to be more than I can manage," I says.

"I thought you was the warlord of the Eleventh?" O'Shea says. "What brought you over here to your old stamping ground in the wee hours of the night?"

Before I can answer Rourke says, "Exactly what time was it that you stopped in here?"

"I'd say midnight."

Rourke gives me the nod and I go on.

"Mabel's already here. She's sitting in my chair behind my desk."

"At midnight? What was she doing here at midnight?"

"Same thing as me, I suppose."

"But you ain't told us what that was," O'Shea says. "Why was you here, that hour, and not home in bed with your wife?"

"I been running around all day, here and there, all wound up."

"Here and there?" O'Shea says, ready to start digging.

"Wanted a quiet minute before going home?" Rourke says, cutting his partner off. "I can understand that. You can understand that, can't you, Frank?" He looks at me. "So you were here with Milton—Mabel—just chewing the fat?"

"That's right."

"About what?"

"She was having trouble in her personal life and was very upset."

"She say what kind of trouble?"

"She didn't really confide in me, but I got the idea she was having a relationship with—"

"Intimate relationship?" Rourke says.

"That's the impression I got. Intimate enough for her to decide to tell her boyfriend the truth."

O'Shea glanced at Rourke.

"You say she told you that she told the man she was having sex with that she'd once been a he?"

"No, she didn't tell me that. I thought she was going to tell me something like that, but thought better of it and said we should go home."

"What time?" Rourke asked.

"One o'clock. Around one o'clock."

"See anything on the street?"

"Nothing. Not a soul. This ain't a very busy avenue even during business hours. No bars up or down the street for at least four blocks each way."

"So, any activity on the street you would have noticed?"

"I would."

"But you didn't," O'Shea said.

"I heard a car start up. I was locking the door."

"You see the car?"

"All I saw was the headlights wash across the door. Then Halstead was pushing me from behind, yelling for me to get down."

"And the shots?"

"I heard the shots. Three shots. Rapid fire. I went through the window with Mabel on top of me."

"You got any cuts on your hands or face?" O'Shea asks me.

"What? I don't know."

I look down at my hands. There's blood on them. I touch my face.

"My blood? Her blood?" I says.

"As long as you don't feel any cuts or bleeding, we might as well finish up here. Okay?" Rourke says. "We'll have a medic check you out in a minute."

"That's okay with me," I says, staring at my hands. "Could I have a wet towel, though. Get this . . ."

I stop right there at the word, not wanting to say it again. Mabel's blood on my hands. My friend's blood on my hands.

"You want to go on?" Rourke asks.

"Sure. But I don't know what more I can tell you."

O'Shea brings me a towel after wetting it from the jug in the water cooler.

"Well, you already told us a lot," Rourke says. "You told us somebody was staking you out. The car was parked over on the side street and started its strafing run when Mabel and you come out of the storefront."

"They fired when you stopped to lock the door," O'Shea says.

"Maybe whoever did it was stalking you," Rourke says. "Followed you from someplace. Where were you before you come here?"

"In my new office across the street from Schaller's Pump over to the Eleventh."

"You got a hell of a lot of places of business," Rourke says.

"You left there, what time?" O'Shea asks.

"Eleven-thirty. About eleven-thirty," I says.

"Everything all right at Schaller's?" Rourke asks.

"Buck Bailey got drunk and tried to start a fight with me."

"Tried to start?" O'Shea says.

"It didn't last long. He slipped and bumped his nose on the bar."

"What was you fighting about?"

"It wasn't a fight exactly, more like kids shoving in the playground," I says, not telling the exact truth and not really sure why I'm not telling the exact truth.

"So what was you shoving about?"

"Bailey accused Canarias and me of not giving him the welcome he thinks he deserves in the Twenty-seventh."

"And it ended there? No threats of more to come?" Rourke asks.

"If there was any, I didn't hear them. I left before it went any farther."

"So, before that?" O'Shea says.

"Before Schaller's Pump?"

"Yeah, before that."

"I was at my Eleventh Ward office."

"Alone?" O'Shea asks.

"No. Somebody was helping me."

"Who would that be?"

"Shaftoe."

"Who?"

"Robert Shaftoe."

"Old friend?"

"No, a new associate. You heard the name?"

"Sounds familiar," O'Shea says. "But I can't place it."

"There's an old nursery rhyme about a kid named Bobby Shaftoe," Rourke says.

"What are you talking about?" O'Shea says, showing a little irritation which he does when somebody drops a remark he don't understand.

Rourke half recites, half sings the old nursery rhyme.

"Bobby Shaftoe went to sea.
Silver buckles on his knee.
He'll come home and marry me.
Pretty Bobby Shaftoe.
Bobby Shaftoe's fine and fair.
Combing down his auburn hair.
He's my friend for evermore.
Pretty Bobby Shaftoe."

"What the hell is that all about?" O'Shea says as though shocked and dismayed that a partner of his should be reciting Mother Goose verses.

Rourke smiles. "The kiddies like them," he says.

"My God, you'll be dressing up like Santa Claus next," O'Shea says. He turns to me. "You want to tell us anything else about before you got here?"

I shake my head.

"So, go on. After you heard the shots."

"Mabel pushed me through the door window. The alarm went off. I was on my face. There was broken glass all around. Mabel was on top of me. The next thing I know Penny Tucker's pulling me away from Mabel."

They both take a step back as though agreeing there's nothing more to be squeezed out of me.

"You want to call Mary? Anybody?" Rourke asks.

"I don't know if I should wake her up," I says.

"It's two-thirty, Jimmy. I got a feeling she may be awake and worrying," Rourke says.

"You're right," I says.

"Your hands is as clean as you're going to get them with that towel," Rourke says, taking it away from me.

I pick up the phone and punch in my home number. The

receiver on the other end's picked up right away, like Mary's been sitting right on it.

"Jimmy?" she says, her voice full of fear.

"I'm okay, Mary."

"If you were going to be this late, why didn't you call me?" she asks, immediately switching to a hurt and angry tone.

"Well, I should've called you, sweetheart. I should've called you the minute I thought I was going to be late, but I didn't want to wake you."

"You not being here keeps me awake," she says, still running with her angry relief. Then she switches again. "You're sure you're all right?"

"Yes, I am."

"But somebody isn't all right?"

"Mabel Halstead's dead, Mary."

"Oh, my God. How?"

"Gunshot."

"Where?"

"Outside the storefront."

"In the Twenty-seventh?"

"Yes," I says. "I'll be home inside an hour, Mary. Maybe sooner."

I hang up. Mary's acting like a nurse in an ER doing triage, asking all these curt questions with one or two words, which I don't want to go through again.

The medic from the examiner's office comes in and looks me over.

"How'd you do it?" he says. "How'd you go through a glass door and not get cut up?"

I look up and see O'Shea and Rourke looking at me in this wary way cops look when they're wondering if somebody ain't altogether just an innocent bystander.

Twenty-two

Mary's not the kind of woman that cries at the drop of a dime. She's been a nurse for a long time and seen so many pitiful things and so much pain and suffering that she's got ways to defend against them. Besides, when I get home, Kathleen's up and looking at me with big eyes, sensing, like kids and animals do, that something ain't quite right.

Mary hugs me a little tighter than usual. The kind of hug that means to protect me from anything bad that might ever come my way.

After we tuck Kathleen back in and I give Alfie another pat on the head to let the old dog know that I'm really all right, Mary and me go into our bedroom.

It's after four in the morning but I don't feel like going to bed because I know I ain't going to sleep a wink.

"Get into your pajamas and under the covers anyway," Mary says. "If you can't sleep at least you can rest your body."

I do like she says and she gets into bed beside me.

Then she starts to cry.

Sometime around dawn I fall asleep after all.

*   *   *

I know the drill good enough to know that the interrogation on the site is only the first and there could be a lot more, so I ain't surprised when I get a call from Bill Malloy, the chief of detectives at the precinct which serves the Twenty-seventh, asking me to come down and clear up a couple of things.

I don't know Malloy all that well, having only met him once or twice, here and there, but the word is that he's a fair-minded cop who rarely cut a deal for hisself or anybody else. And the times he did cut a deal or give an edge was because there was two wrongs he figured canceled themselves out but one of the people involved needed his help more than the other. Or there was two rights, and he had to choose which was righter.

He's a slender guy what looks no more like a cop than I do. In fact less. He gets up from behind his desk and reaches out to shake my hand.

"I've heard a lot about you, Mr. Flannery."

"Nothing good, I hope," I says, using the old joking formula with the police, hoping they ain't going to say you're wrong about that.

"Detectives O'Shea and Rourke filed their report. There's a couple of things here I'd like to double-check with you."

"There's something I'd like to ask you, too," I says.

"Go ahead."

"How come O'Shea and Rourke caught the call?"

"They're headquarters men," Malloy says. "Every precinct call goes through headquarters. You know that. They picked it up off the screen and tapped Captain Buntley, night watch, for permission to roll on it. Are you complaining about the special treatment you're getting, Flannery?"

So it ain't "Mr." anymore.

"I just wondered if they were keeping a special eye on me or my ward for some reason unbeknownst to me."

"As far as I know it was nothing but pure chance," Malloy says. "Now, my turn?"

Reading from a report, he starts asking me questions related to what I already told O'Shea and Rourke.

I know the way it works, so I don't object. Cops ask the same questions over and over again, make you tell your story over and over again, for two reasons. One, they might be able to build a case on some small contradiction or inconsistency. Two, they might jog a memory loose.

"You know anybody out to get you, Flannery? You get any hate mail recently? Any threats?"

"I suppose like anybody who ever deals with the public on a regular basis, I got my share of people what don't like me very much. I suppose I've even got a couple of enemies just like I bet you got a couple of enemies."

He nods and smiles.

"I might even know a few who'd like to see me dead, but I don't know anybody who'd try to make it happen," I says.

"It's usually somebody you wouldn't think would make it happen who makes it happen," he says. "So, you haven't told me. Have you had any hate mail?"

"I got a pile of it."

"More than usual?"

"More than when I was taking care of the Twenty-seventh," I says.

"You save it?"

"No, I usually dump it. I don't even read it through once I see what it's going to be about."

"So, it doesn't scare you?"

"Well, yeah, it scares me, but I don't know what I can do about it."

"You ever save any of it?"

I shake my head.

"You happen to have any on your desk or in your files now?"

"Some."

"How come, if you usually trash it, that you've still got some?"

"I got a new assistant lately. He advised me to take such mail a little more seriously. At least let him vet it."

"He say why?"

"Mentioned that it might be useful if anybody tried to carry out a threat."

"He got a name?"

"Robert Shaftoe."

Malloy leans forward and makes a note of the name on the corner of his blotter.

"You mind if I send over a man to collect that mail and look it over?"

"You mean I should've been taking it seriously?"

"I mean you never know. Also, sometimes, a letter we get from one place links up with a letter we get from another place."

He stands up.

"Well, anything I can do to help you learn the neighborhoods, you just let me know, will you?"

We shake hands and I go to the door.

"Oh, by the way, I understand you had a fight with Buck Bailey and Pat Connell over to Schaller's Pump last night."

"Bailey had a few too many," I says.

"Also a bad temper. That's what got him in trouble before."

"I don't think he'd carry it that far again," I says.

"How far is that?"

"Far enough to try and kill me."

"Wouldn't you say he could have more reason to kill you than he did to beat those two men to death? Watch your back."

I leave, thinking about the people I know who'd want me dead and could find the balls to make it happen.

How far back do I have to go? I mean I had my quarrels and little run-ins going back to when I was a kid in the playgrounds, things you practically totally forget about a month after they happen. But nowadays people with automatic weapons walk into business offices and doctors' offices and post offices and restaurants and start shooting for some injury, real or imagined, that was done to them, a year, five years, ago.

So, it's perfectly possible that some kid I kicked in the knee when I was ten is a forty-year-old man who's been brooding about it all these years and one night decides he's going to do me in.

There's probably one or two I work with down in the sewers who take exception to my personality or the color of my hair, but that's about as doubtful as the first proposition.

Chances are, if somebody was coming after me, it would be something to do with politics. I got to figure that for every person I ever helped there could be another person dislikes me because of what I done.

So looking at the people I met or remet recently, I'm thinking of Buck Bailey most of all.

Also, because of the confrontation I have with Lundatos up at Club Fed, there's an outside chance he put a hit out on me. I don't want to be accused of political incorrectness but it's a well-known fact that Greeks is very passionate and jealous people.

Janet Canarias ain't in her office or her storefront. I call the morgue and find out she's down there making the official identification.

By the time I get there, she's through with it and looking grim and uncertain.

"You all right?" I asks.

"Ah, Jimmy," she says, as though she expected more from me than something as ordinary as that.

I put my arms around her and she holds on for a minute, then breaks away.

"Cup of coffee?" she says.

"There's a place around the corner," I says.

When we get to the diner she orders coffee and I order milk.

"You got a stomachache?" she asks.

"You think I could be getting an ulcer?" I asks.

"Go see a doctor, Jimmy. No need to suffer if you don't have to suffer."

"Well, it ain't that bad. Only now and then I get a little nervous stomach."

"I don't wonder we don't all have nervous stomachs," she says.

When the coffee comes, she takes a swallow. "That was very hard for me, Jimmy. Very hard."

"You weren't having . . ."

I don't finish what I start to say.

"A relationship with Mabel?"

"None of my business," I says.

"It'd seem sort of right for me to get intimate with Mabel,

wouldn't it? After all I work both sides of the street, like they say. With Mabel I could resolve the conflict in my own heart. I'd have a woman with some of a man's sensibilities and a man with a woman's body. Jackpot."

"Hey," I says, telling her to come down off the pain and sorrow.

"No, Jimmy, there was no chemistry between Mabel and me. Just good, good friends."

"More precious than gold," I says.

"You know the poem?"

"I didn't know it was from a poem," I says. "It's just something my mother—God rest her soul—used to say."

"How did you feel about Mabel, Jimmy?"

"Same as you, except I knew her pretty good when she was Milton Halstead, one of the best cops I ever met. As pretty and feminine as she was, I couldn't ever stop seeing her as a man. Even the way she stepped in and helped me out with a couple of bone-breakers kept that opinion of her alive. And at the end—I'm not saying another person, man or woman, wouldn't've put themselves in harm's way to push me—it was a cop's instincts that got her moving and saved my life."

"You have any idea who was out to get you?"

"I can't even make up a decent field of probables. There's some very long shots but I figure your committeeman in your ward for the front runner."

"Bailey? I don't think he's got the *cojones* to take a shot at you."

"He had the guts to beat up on your friends so bad he killed them," I said.

"He's served some time since then. He sees himself rising

in the party. He's got more to lose now. I can't see him trying to kill you because you put him away ten years ago."

"I can't see him coming straight at me, either. But I can see him getting half-bagged and, maybe alone, maybe with that friend of his, sitting in a car in the wee smalls, sharing the tail end of a pint, and bragging about what they could do to me the next time they had the chance."

Janet sits there looking doubtful.

"I know it's a stretch, but what else have I got to go on at the minute?" I says.

"How are you going to start checking it out?" Janet says.

"I'm going to go over to Schaller's Pump and have a talk with Harry Fannon, the bartender, first of all."

It's the slow hour between dinner and the evening crowd. Harry Fannon's behind the wood wiping a glass with a clean towel, making a jeweler's art out of it. Holding it up to the light. Removing every stain and smudge.

He sees me coming and pulls a Vernor's ginger ale from the refrigerator.

I hold up a hand to stop him.

"I ain't going to be here long enough to drink it, Harry," I says, putting a fiver on the bar.

He glances at it and looks quizzical.

"Forgot to leave you a tip last night," I says.

"Not required, not expected," he says, not touching the fin.

"I'm sorry about the fuss."

"Not your fault. I was standing right here watching it all. Bailey was out of line . . ." He leaves a long pause and then adds, "again."

"Well, I shouldn't've let it happen anyway."

"What could you've done? He wasn't giving you any room."

"I got to figure out something I can do about them two."

"I'd say so. They're carrying a lot of bad feelings against you."

"They stay after I left?" I asks.

"For an hour maybe."

"Having more to drink?"

"All they could manage. Some of the other boys here last night set them up. Claimed they was celebration drinks for the way Bailey beat up on you, taught you what was what and who was who."

"Did what?" I says, surprised at such a thing.

"They was pulling Bailey's leg. Making fun of him. Making him a goat. He didn't know no better."

"How about Connell?"

"He knew what was going on but he didn't clue Bailey in that they were making a fool of him. He was downing the free drinks, too."

"They make any threats against me?"

Fannon makes believe the glass he's working on has a stubborn spot, deciding what he should or shouldn't say.

"Come on, Harry, I know they're regular customers and I know bartenders don't like to bad-mouth regulars. But I'm going to be around more than a little and maybe I'll get to be a regular."

"Ginger ale?" Fannon says, but he's grinning. "It was just pissin' in the wind, Jimmy. You know how drunks get. Especially when a bunch of jackasses are egging them on."

"So some threats were made."

"The usual. How next time they'd tear your head off, rip your balls off, and otherwise rearrange your anatomy."

"They?"

"Connell wasn't going to let Bailey get the best of it, what he'd do to you the next time. They kept on topping one another and the rest of the bar was laughing."

"That's all?"

"Well, it went on for a while. I can't remember every damn thing he said."

"Did he mention doing anything to me with anything other than his fists and feet?"

"What the hell are you talking about, Jimmy? He just made the usual threats like a kid or a drunk'll make."

I don't want to lead him into remembering something he don't remember on his own. I don't want to tell him the reason I'm prodding him is to find out if Bailey or Connell mentioned anything about guns in their threats.

"I don't know. Maybe they said something about doing worse to me than just beating me up."

Fannon's been a bartender for a long time and he ain't no fool. He narrows his eyes as though seeing me better'll make him hear what I'm saying without saying it.

"Like they might blow your brains out?" he asks.

"Well, did they say anything like that?"

"It was all just drunken brag, Jimmy."

"Did they say anything like that?"

"Well, yeah, they did. Bailey said something like that."

"Anything else?"

"Has something bad happened which you ain't telling me?" he asks.

"It was on the local news."

"I watch the television with half an eye and I don't even bother listening with half an ear."

"Somebody took a shot at me last night."

"Jesus, Mary and Joseph," Fannon says. "You okay?"

"I didn't get hit but Mabel Halstead got it."

"Do I know the lady?"

"Probably not. But she got killed."

"And you think Bailey and Connell might've done it?"

"I don't know. I'm just picking through the garbage because, right now, I don't know what else I can do. Well, thanks, Harry."

"Hey, Flannery," he says, as I start to walk away. "Pick up your fiver."

When I don't reach for it right away he pushes it closer to me and says, "You want to, add it to any floral tribute you're gonna send the lady."

Twenty-three

It's nine o'clock before I wake up.

Mary's been up a couple of hours, getting Kathleen dressed and fed and off to school on the bus.

So we have one of our long talks while I eat the breakfast she makes for me.

"Did she have any relatives?" she asks.

"She may have told me she had a couple of brothers or sisters. Maybe some aunts, uncles and cousins. Nephews and nieces. I don't know. She might have told me that. She never talked about her family much that I can remember. I have an idea that any family she had disowned her after she quit being Milton and had the sex-change operation. I could find out from Janet if she knows anything I don't know."

"I could do that for you," Mary says.

"I appreciate the offer, sweetheart, but I think I've got to do this thing for my friend. Try to take some of the confusion out of her death which I couldn't take out of her life."

"I understand," Mary says. "But if you need me to do anything at all, please let me help."

"Yes, I'll do that," I says. "Right now I think I'll go over and talk to Janet."

"She called this morning and said she'd be at her office down in City Hall until one o'clock this afternoon if you wanted her for anything."

"She called this morning?"

"While you were asleep. I didn't want to wake you."

"Will you give her a call for me while I get dressed?" I asks. "Tell her I'll be right down."

When I get to City Hall and the floor where Janet has her official office, I see her walking toward me the way she walks, striding out like a person going somewhere. She starts to hold out her arms when she's a good ways away from me and starts to come at me in a rush. It's like one of them scenes in a moving picture where two lovers come together in a field of flowers.

But we ain't two lovers eager to embrace, we're a couple of old friends seeking comfort in each other because of the violent death of a friend.

We hold each other as people hurry past, giving us the eye.

Janet breaks away, her hands still on my arms, and smiles at me.

"We're an item now, Jimmy."

"The world is full of fools," I says.

"Come on back into my office," Janet says.

"Did Mabel ever talk about her family?"

"A little, now and then. Particularly if she was feeling blue. She'd talk about being a little kid living with her mom and dad, and a brother and sister in . . . in . . . in . . ." She's searching her memory. ". . . in Highland Park."

Highland Park's a very upscale community that stretches along about five miles of the Lake Michigan shoreline. It's maybe twenty-five miles north of downtown Chicago. The Metra makes it there in just over half an hour or you can take the Interstate 94 or U.S. 41 if you want to go by car.

I happen to know about it because Mary went through a period a couple of years back when she thought we needed more culture in our lives. So one summer weekend we drive up there to the Ravinia Festival where some world-class musicians, dancers and actors perform.

"How about lately?" I asks, taking the visitor's chair.

"The best I can do, perhaps, is to try to recall the names of the schools he went to."

"That'd be a help."

She stares out the window, trying to get her memory to bring up some information. But after a couple of minutes she spins back around and says, "What am I doing, wasting time trying to remember? Just a second, Jimmy."

There's a computer monitor on a swivel arm attached to her desk. She brings it around in front of her and slides out a keyboard from under her desk drawer. She pushes a key and something beeps.

"The CPU's in my desk drawer," she says.

"Oh," I says, seeing as how I don't know what she's talking about.

Then I remember Kathleen explaining to me that CPU stands for central processing unit.

"That's a good place for a central processing unit," I says.

Janet looks at me funny, like if I know what's a CPU why do I have to spell it out and not call it a CPU?

The screen's up. She clicks this and clicks that. It makes more noises.

"Okay," she says. "Move your chair around over here."

By the time I shift my chair so I can see the screen over her shoulder, there's something up there, a document headed "Personnel Records."

She taps the keys and comes up with another page headed "Ward Office."

Then she scrolls down past addresses, telephone and fax numbers, and stuff about rent and utilities until she comes to a subheading for "Volunteers" and right there, at the top of a short list, is Mabel Halstead.

"Here we go," Janet says. "Mabel Halstead, current address, 729 North State Street. I don't think that's her home address. I think that's the office she was using when she was selling insurance and brokering stocks for the professional women."

"She could have been sleeping there, too," I says.

"No age," Janet says, and smiles like I smile, both of us thinking that hiding her age was a very feminine thing for Mabel to do.

"Kindergarten through five, Kipling Elementary School, 517 Deerfield Road, Deerfield, Illinois. Shepard Junior High School, grades six through eight, 440 Grove, Deerfield. Deerfield High School. College of Lake County, 1860 First Street, Highland Park, Illinois. United States Army, Vietnam."

"She put that down as an address? Vietnam?" I asks.

"Yes," Janet says.

"What year did he go in?"

"Nineteen sixty-five."

"Right there at the beginning of Johnson's war," I says. "When did he get out?"

"There's no date of discharge, but he went into the Chicago Metropolitan Police Academy in June of 1968."

I do a quick calculation in my head. Fourteen weeks at the academy and twenty-five weeks in-service training at district stations. Ten months. On duty in '69.

"Do you have anything on the precincts he worked in?" I asks.

"The only other entry is a note that says he took a six-month leave of absence in 1987, then resigned before the six months were up."

"Did he put that entry down in your regular information sheet?"

"No, I probably checked with the department," Janet says.

"To see if there was a shadow over his career that forced him out?"

"Standard practice. Everybody gets vetted to one degree or another. You can't be too careful nowadays and friendship doesn't figure into it."

"So, he quits two years short of retirement," I says. "That must've been when he made up his mind to have the operation."

"And he's been Mabel Halstead ever since. Ten years."

We sit there quiet for a long time, each of us in his or her own thoughts about this tall, beautiful woman we knew or thought we knew. Because, actually, we didn't have a clue about how Mabel really thought and felt. She was a helpful presence but the notion that she was a novelty was never altogether out of mind.

"Well," I says, "I think maybe I should try to locate her people and tell them that their . . . child . . . is dead."

"Wait a second, Jimmy. Let me see if I can get a telephone number and an address for you."

She selects a jewel box, one of them containers for a CD, from a line of them between bookends on her desk, opens it up and pops it into a drawer that comes whispering out of her computer at a keystroke.

"White pages for the United States," she says.

"You telling me that little disk has got every telephone number in the country?"

"Well, this one's got all the numbers from the Atlantic seaboard to the Rockies. At least that's what they say. But like everything else, much is promised and less is delivered. Updates aren't sent. Companies fail. Well, you know. Still and all I get a hit about nine times out of ten."

She types in "Illinois," then "Deerfield" and then "Halstead." A short list of four names comes up. One's a post office box, the other three's got addresses.

Janet punches a key, and the printer, a little cream-colored thing no bigger than a lunch box, lights up and starts chugging away.

"They might have an unlisted number," Janet says. "Or, of course, his people might not even be living there anymore."

She hands me the printed sheet and I look it over.

"John J. Halstead," I read out loud, "800 Rosemary Terrace, Deerfield." Then there's another John D. Halstead, on Lake Cook Road. And a Halstead and Son, Plumbing. And this last one just has the name and number but no address.

Janet's tapping away at the keyboard again. The computer in the drawer makes phone dialing sounds. Then there's a little crash of beeps and hisses.

"I'm on," Janet says, more to herself than to me.

"On what?"

"The Web."

More key tapping and I see a screen come up what says "MapBlast!"

Janet types in the address for John J. Halstead. In a minute, maybe a little more, the printer's spitting out a map with a little red cross marking the spot.

She does the same for Kipling Elementary and Shepard Junior High.

So I got these three maps, one of the man's address on Rosemary and one each for the schools, which are both easy walking distance from the house where John J. lives.

"Anything else you can think of?" Janet asks.

"I couldn't even think of what you got already," I says. "I got to start taking some computer lessons from Kathleen."

"Do you want to call those four numbers?" she asks.

When I hesitate she says, "Do you want me to do it?"

"I hate giving people bad news over the phone," I says. "It's very hard, but I'd rather do it face-to-face."

"I understand, but these people may be no relations. His folks may have moved away long ago."

"Okay," I says, reaching for the phone.

I punch in the number for John J. The phone rings several times and then an answering machine kicks in, "You have reached the residence of John J. Halstead. If you wish to leave a message wait for the signal. If you want to reach Halstead and Son, Plumbing, the number is . . ."

The message gets cut off abruptly and a woman's voice, which sounds out of breath, says, "Yes. I'm here."

"I take you away from something?"

"That's all right. I was out in the garden."

"I wanted to speak to Mr. Halstead. I need a plumber and—"

"Oh, well, this isn't the shop. You must've got the numbers mixed up. The shop number's—"

"I got it right here in the book," I says, interrupting her, acting like I'm embarrassed for making the mistake. "I'm really sorry I got you out of your garden on such a nice day."

"Well," she says, with a little laugh in her voice, "I can go right back to it. It's not far."

"I used to live in Deerfield before I moved to Highland Park," I says, telling a white lie.

"Did you?"

"Went to Kipling Elementary."

"My children went to Kipling," she says. "Did you go to Shepard Junior?"

"Well, yes I did."

"And Deerfield High, too?" she asks, with this wonder in her voice that people get when a coincidence happens in their life, like there's something amazing about it, that two people who lived in a fairly small town should have gone to the same schools.

"I think I knew a couple of Halstead brothers at Kipling and Shepard," I says. "Johnny and Milton."

"Did you?" she says, and now I hear some wariness where there was nothing but a kind of innocent eagerness before.

I think maybe I tried something to establish a connection there that gave her some kind of warning.

"Johnny? You mean Jack. We always called my youngest Jack."

"It's been a long time," I says. "My memory ain't always so good. Just out of curiosity, did I get Milton right?"

"No, you didn't," she says. "You say you've got the shop number?"

"Yes, I do."

"Good-bye, then," she says, and hangs up.

I hang up the phone, wondering if I should call the shop and go any further with the search. But then I think that if I do, and the family compares notes around the dinner table I might be causing some nice people some unnecessary anxiety and concern.

"I think that's them," I says. "Something I said pushed her alarm button and she cut me off."

"Are you going out to Deerfield?" Janet asks.

"I think I will."

"If there was no connection between Mabel and her family anymore, maybe it'd be just as well to leave it alone," Janet says.

"No matter how bad feelings was between them, they'd want to know their son and brother died when Mabel died."

I go over to Bochos Elementary in the neighborhood what they call SuHu in the Eighth. It's on my way to Deerfield.

I catch Cora Esper teaching her last class of the day.

I sit in the back while Cora explains gerunds, which is what you call a verb while it's acting like a noun. So at least some of what she taught me stuck. Though what good it does me I ain't yet found out.

She dismisses the class and comes over and sits down in one of them chairs with the big arms like the one I'm sitting in.

"I would've been over sooner, Cora, but there's been some things taking up my time. A friend of mine got killed."

"I'm sorry to hear that, Jimmy. This thing for me. It's not that important."

"No, it's important, all right."

"I mean compared to somebody getting killed. Was it a house invasion or a mugging?"

"She got in the way of a couple of bullets meant for me."

Cora gasped like I'd hit her in the face.

"You don't suppose it's because of this thing I asked you to do?"

"I don't think things are so bad that somebody on a school council will kill somebody for asking about some books getting banned."

"Then you went over to a meeting?"

"Sure, and spotted the troublemaker right away, because I'd had some trouble with him before. It was ten years ago."

"Joseph Asbach?"

"That's him. You know him, too?"

"I've seen more of him than I've wanted to see," she says. "Prowling around the school. Looking into the library. He seems to be a man with a lot of time on his hands."

"I think he's one of them people who believes that all you got to do to be a leader is find a parade and get in front of it."

"Unless he's got some personal interest, what's he get out of it?"

"Some power and maybe some money. You get a cause like banning books and start an organization to protect the children from dirty words and naked ladies. You file a non-profit with the state. You send out a mailer and ask for contributions. You'd be surprised how much money you can make and how careless everybody is about checking up on organizations like that."

"So much effort is put into all the wrong places," Cora says.

"Everybody's got a favorite issue," I says. "One person's casual comment is another person's cause. So you seen Asbach around. You ever talk to him?"

"I went to one of their meetings and confronted him before I brought it up to you."

"What did he say at the time?"

"He tried to hit on me. When I told him I was married he got mean and cute."

"How's that?"

"Made some cracks about did I like to read dirty books."

"It's a thing with him. He's one of them men never grows up when it comes to women. Funny thing is them types seem to do all right with the ladies."

"There are a lot of lonely, hungry ladies out there and he's not bad-looking. Maybe that's why he has trouble understanding no. Even after I made it clear that I had no interest he flirted with me when he was with another woman."

"Where was this?"

"In a restaurant in the Loop. The Napoli. I couldn't believe my eyes. He's with this big, beautiful woman and he's making faces at me, as though he thinks I should realize what I missed turning him down, a man hot enough to attract a woman like her."

"What night was this?"

"Friday. Friday before last."

I think that over for a minute. I know there's plenty of big, beautiful women in Chicago, but I see Asbach giving the eye to Mabel, chatting her up at Schaller's Pump the night I was named committeeman, so you don't have to be a fortune-teller to figure that the woman Cora saw Asbach with was Mabel.

I'm wondering if he knows what's happened to her. It was on the television and all over the newspapers, somebody making an attempt on a committeeman's life. I wonder if I'm going to be seeing him at the funeral service. I even wonder should I give him a call and tell him his friend is dead, in case for some reason he ain't heard about it.

"Jimmy?" Cora says, bringing me around. "You all right?"

"Sure. My mind's wandering. I got a lot on my plate."

"Too much, perhaps?"

"Well, I just stopped by to tell you I ain't . . ."

"Haven't," she says.

"I've been forgetting a lot of what you taught me."

"Just keep practicing the right way and it'll all come back. Anytime you want a refresher just come and take a seat. You don't have to register or anything like that."

"Anyway I wanted to tell you I haven't forgotten what you asked me to look into for you."

"It doesn't seem very important compared to losing a friend through violence."

"Oh, it's important," I says. "I couldn't walk you through the steps from one to another, but I know they're there. People trying to force other people to do what they want them to do, or else. So, I just wanted to tell you I haven't forgotten."

We leave the classroom and go out into the corridor.

A school feels very funny when it's empty or nearly empty. There's a smell of oil and chalk dust that brings back memories of when I was a kid.

I see a sign up on the wall where two corridors meet what says "Library." When we get there I look to my left. There's a man coming out the library. He looks at me. It's Asbach.

Cora sees him too.

"There's just the man I want to see," I says. "I'll keep you posted."

"Thank you, Jimmy," Cora says, and hurries off like she'd

just as soon not meet up with Asbach again, at least not right that minute.

"Hey, Mr. Asbach," I call out, because after spotting me, he's turned away and started down the hall.

He stops and turns to face me as I approach.

"I thought it was you but I couldn't be sure," he says. "Taking lessons from our pretty Miss Esper?" He puts a suggestive little spin on it.

"Mrs. Esper," I says.

"Well, Ms. if you want to be politically correct," he says, giving me a little bit of the old curly lip.

"I wouldn't ever want it said that I wasn't politically correct. It's the interpretation of what is and what ain't that we might have a little trouble with."

"Still leading the charge against what you call censorship?" he says.

"I'm just lending a hand. It ain't my special cause."

"That's right, you're the committeeman, soon to be the alderman, of the Eleventh, aren't you?"

"I was surprised to see you at the celebration over to Schaller's Pump when O'Meara made the announcement."

"I've got friends here and there," he says. "I was invited."

"I just didn't think you'd be interested in seeing me getting passed the ball."

"Bailey was named to replace you in the Twenty-seventh, don't forget," he says.

"Ah. So you're a friend of Bailey's."

"I know him."

"I saw you that night with my office manager and administrative assistant," I says, watching his expression like a hawk.

"Yes?"

"You know who I mean?"

"Yes, Mabel Halstead."

"She didn't tell you that she worked for me?"

"Oh, yes, she told me," he says. "But we didn't talk about work very much."

"Didn't?"

"When we went out together."

"Haven't you seen her lately?"

"I don't think who I see or don't see is any of your business."

"I didn't say it was. I was just making conversation about a mutual friend, here. There any reason why we shouldn't?"

"No specific reason. I have a general prohibition against talking about my personal life to virtual strangers."

"That's fair enough."

"What's this all about anyway?" he asks. "You didn't chase me down the corridor just to talk about Mabel."

"Well, actually, I did. I wanted to find out how close you two were before I tell you something you apparently ain't heard."

"About Mabel?"

"I don't know how to say it any easier. She's dead."

He looks at me for a long time, staring into my eyes without blinking, until I start feeling uncomfortable.

"You all right?" I says.

"Do you dislike me so much you'd tell me this sort of dirty lie?"

"It's no lie. I'm afraid it's the truth."

"How? When? Where?"

"Killed by gunfire Friday night in front of my ward office in the Twenty-seventh."

"Who did it?"

"We don't know. It was a drive-by. The police are looking into it. You want me to keep you informed of any progress?"

"I'll keep myself informed," he says, turning away from me like he's got no reason to keep on talking to me.

He don't ask me if she's going to be laid out or where she's going to be buried or if there's going to be a memorial service.

Twenty-four

Finding Halstead and Son, Plumbing, ain't very difficult at all. As I'm driving down the main street I see a sign painted on the side of a brick building on a corner with the name and a hand with a pointing finger. Also it says established 1927, so the Halsteads've been plumbers for quite a while, father to son, father to son.

I wonder if Milton's father was proud or disappointed when he decided to become a cop. After all he had another son to carry on the business.

The shop ain't right out there on the street but set way back on a big lot with several upper-canopy shade trees. It looks more like a smithy than a plumbing shop and I realize that's exactly what it must've been once upon a time.

I drive through the entrance between these well-trimmed low hedges and park on the gravel next to a truck with the same information painted on the side.

The store's more like a shed with big windows on either side of the door.

Inside there's all sorts of fittings and commodes and sinks and other items, and a counter with a line of catalogs.

The man behind it is studying something in his hands. He looks up over the tops of his glasses. I can see he's too young to be the father, so it's probably the other son, Mabel's brother.

"I was just about to close," he says, very mildly as though it ain't going to be any trouble at all to help me if it won't take too long. "You need a part?"

"Are you Mr. Halstead?"

"No, my name's Harry Cope."

I always find that a man who gives me his full name when asked is a friendly man.

"My name's Jimmy Flannery. Is either of the Halsteads around?"

"Either?"

"I thought there was a father and son, like the sign says."

"Oh, no. There's a son all right but he's not in the business with John. He's a lawyer back east. New York or New Jersey. Maybe Pennsylvania."

"Just the one son?"

"There was another but he was killed in Vietnam."

"So that's just an old sign nobody ever bothered to change."

"Well, I'm the son-in-law. Is there something I can do for you?"

He's getting a little wary, a little suspicious. I can see his smile and the rest of his face closing up. He gets up off the stool. In a second he's going to be asking me to leave the shop because he's closing up.

But then he looks over my shoulder and sort of relaxes. I hear gravel crunching outside the door.

When I turn around an older man in work clothes is just laying his hand on the door latch and a young woman in jacket and jeans steps around him when he opens the door and comes in first.

She smiles and says, "Hello," the way shopkeepers greet people, with a little lift like a question, everybody a potential customer.

The old man's caught something in Harry Cope's attitude and he don't give me a hello.

"What is it, Harry?" he says.

"I don't know yet. This fella hasn't said what it is he wants."

"I had some information for a John Halstead who lives here in Deerfield."

"What kind of information?"

"Personal. I wouldn't want to deliver it to the wrong Halstead. I notice there's four in the telephone book."

"That's right. Even another John Halstead. So, how are you going to know which is the right one?" he asks, assuming that I got the whole name right. That I'm supposed to deliver some information to a John Halstead and not some other.

"The John Halstead I was looking for has a son who lived in Chicago," I says.

His face is telling me everything and I'm aware that the young woman, who went behind the counter next to Harry, who I figure is her husband, stiffens up and stands there like she's waiting to take a punch.

"I've got no son living in Chicago," Halstead. "I've got a son in New York and that's all I've got."

He doesn't say that the second son died in Vietnam the way Harry told me. That's the way the father wanted the story of the second son known and Harry was honoring that.

Halstead was playing it differently. He figures a stranger, even a stranger with a message, didn't have to know a thing about any second son.

"So you wouldn't have a son who was a cop in Chicago?" I says.

"No, I wouldn't. Anything else I can do for you?"

"I can't think of anything."

"Have a nice day," he says, and opens the door for me.

On the way to my car I can hear voices raised from the shop behind me and by the time I get to my car the woman's running after me.

I turn around as she runs up to me, her face showing all the fear that's in her after what I said.

"What about this police officer in Chicago?"

"Well, he stopped being a police officer."

"I know, I know. What happened to him?"

I glance over her shoulder and can see the old man standing in the open door with his son-in-law standing behind him.

"He stopped being a him," I says.

"I know that too," she says very softly.

"She was shot and killed," I says.

Tears fill her eyes and run down her cheeks.

"Tell me," she says.

So I tell her some, a lot but not all, about me and Mabel and how she worked for me and how she did so much good for people, and how she got shot protecting me.

"Will your father want to do something about the funeral and the burial?"

She shakes her head. "Oh, no. He might not even want to

hear what I've got to tell him now that you've told me. He tells everybody he thinks has a right to know that Milton died an honorable death in combat."

"Well she did. That's exactly what Mabel did," I says.

Twenty-five

When I get back to Chicago I call Mary and tell her I might be late for supper.

I don't know what I hope to accomplish but I feel like I got to have a face-to-face with Bailey.

First I find Janet Canarias because I want another pair of eyes watching his reactions while I accuse him, which is what I feel like doing and which is the only thing I can think to do, a crime like this without eyewitnesses or anything to hang a hat on.

I find him in the office he's rented over a pizza parlor. The smell of tomato paste and anchovies fills the stairwell and I'm getting hungry just walking up the steps.

His office has a pane of pebbled glass set in the door. His name and title has been painted on the outside and is already showing signs of wear and tear because he couldn't have spent much on the sign painter.

When I knock he immediately says, "Come in."

I open the door and let Janet go in first.

He's got a pair of black eyes from the busted nose I give

him. Some strips of plaster are holding the bone in place. He gets to his feet fast and puts his hand over his nose like he expects that I'm going to hit him again. Like a kid minding his manners he sticks out his hand to me and waves at the only other chair in the room, asking Janet to sit down.

Then he's stuck about what he should do next.

I have an idea that he'd like to toss us out but curiosity, one, and the kind of hospitality I read the Tuaregs in the desert offer their worst enemies, two, has got him confused. Not that he'd know a Tuareg if he met one.

"So why don't you take my chair, Flannery?" he says.

"No, I'm okay. I'll just rest myself on the edge of the desk. You sit down where you belong."

When we're all settled like three old pals about to chew the fat, Janet and me just look at him. We don't say anything, we just look at him.

He's no fool. He knows we're doing a number on him but he don't know what that number might be.

"You got a reason for coming to see me?" he says.

"Well, Ms. Canarias and me happened to be talking about this and that last week and we decided that we'd been neglectful about our good manners."

Janet picks it up right away like we'd rehearsed it. "We've never come to welcome you to the Twenty-seventh."

Bailey smiles a big smile and takes a breath. "Oh, well, that's very nice of you. I wish you gave me some notice. I'd've laid on some refreshment."

"That's okay," I says.

"We could go downstairs, maybe have a glass of wine," he says. "That's right, you don't drink, do you, Flannery?" Like that fact puts my manhood in doubt.

"How about you, Bailey? You still drink?"

"What? Oh, sure, I have a little something now and then. A glass of red with dinner. A beer. Maybe a highball every now and then. But I don't drink like I used to drink."

"That's good," I says.

"Drinking got me in a lot of trouble," he says, smiling at me like we were sharing the memory of some of the things young men do when they tie on the bag down at the tavern.

"No more all-nighters, then? No more drinking into the wee smalls with a friend?"

"No, nothing at all like that anymore," he says.

"Not even with your old buddy Connell?"

The smile leaves Bailey's face. He looks from me to Janet and from Janet to me, his eyes getting narrow with new suspicion.

"What's this all about, Flannery? You'll forgive me if I don't believe you come here to welcome me and wish me well. So what did you come here for?"

"Mostly to see if you were settled in. Mostly to see if you got enough going here in the Twenty-seventh to occupy your time." I stand up. "I still keep an eye out in the Twenty-seventh. In the Eleventh, too. I got people who keep an eye out for me. One of them comes and tells me that you and your friend Connell tied on a big one after I left Schaller's Pump."

"Well, this is a possibility. So what?" He stands up, too. "So what happened the other night, Flannery, that brings you over here giving me the old one-eye? Don't keep on playing me like I was a trout."

"You know Mabel Halstead?" I says.

"Sure, I know that freak. Not as good as you do, but I know that freak."

"That freak is dead," Janet says in a very soft voice.

"What? What're you talking about?"

"Somebody took some shots at me when I was leaving Ms. Canarias's storefront and Mabel threw herself in the way."

"Jesus, Mary and Joseph," Bailey says, sitting back down and acting like a man who has truly been caught off guard by bad news. "Hold it, hold it, hold it. You're here because you think I had something to do with it?"

Janet stands up. We're ready to go.

Bailey stands up again. He's so upset there's tears in his eyes.

"You ever going to let me live it down, Flannery? You, too," he says, looking at Janet but not calling her by name. "I was a drunk when I done what I done. I was ten years younger and a hundred years dumber. I never meant to kill those men."

"Don't you even remember their names?" Janet says.

"Sure, I remember their names. Roger Spencer and Harold Frye. You think I'm ever going to forget their names? You think I'm ever going to forget what I done? I ain't asking you to give me a little goddam pity. I'm just telling you I wake in the night praying I could take it all back. I served nearly ten years, Flannery. Okay? Maybe you don't figure it was enough. I ain't going to argue that. I'm only saying you can let up on me a little because I don't let up on myself."

"You're forgetting something," I says. "You're still a drunk."

He don't even hear me, he just goes right on.

"I didn't expect you to kiss me on the cheek when they give me the Twenty-seventh the way old Delvin give it to you. The way O'Meara and Buckey just handed you the Eleventh. I didn't expect to set up shop in your old office or expect a helping hand. All I want is for you to give me the benefit of the doubt when I tell you that I changed, that I'm trying to put all that behind me. All I want is for you to treat me like a human being."

"Like a human being?" Janet says. "Not a freak like that Mabel Halstead?"

We leave him standing there, a man trapped in his own upbringing, his own prejudices. Maybe he wants to change but the old trash comes out of his mouth every time he opens it, giving the lie to every claim of rehabilitation he makes.

Downstairs, Janet says, "Did you learn anything?"

"Unless he's the best actor since Cagney stood on the roof of that refinery and burned to death, it looks to me like Bailey don't know anything at all about what happened the other night."

"I wasn't really hoping for much anyway," she says. "I didn't expect to be able to read his mind or make him break down and confess."

"Neither did I," I says. "But now the word's out."

"What word's that?"

"That Jimmy Flannery ain't going to stand by and let somebody else clean up the murder of a friend."

That night I get a call at home.

"Jimmy Flannery here," I says.

"This is John Halstead."

"Yes, sir?"

"Can you tell me where my son's body is?"

"At the police morgue."

"I want to move him to a mortuary."

"You can claim the body anytime you want," I says.

"I'll do it first thing in the morning," he says.

"Will you be burying her here?" I asks.

"I'll be having his body cremated and his ashes scattered here in Deerfield."

"If you're going to have a service, I'd like to be there."

"There won't be any service," he says.

We're both silent for a minute.

Then he says, "Did Milton really save your life?"

"Yes, she did, sir," I says.

Twenty-six

Pescaro and me go way back. I met him when he was a detective three in the Twenty-seventh and now he's the chief of Homicide down at headquarters.

I knew him when he ate pastrami with warm pickles which the deli man heated up for him in the steamer. He's still eating pastrami sandwiches but he ain't got the time to go out and get a sandwich with steamed pickles. He's eating his sandwich at his desk when I walk in on him per his request which he left on both my answering machines and with Mary at home.

"You got warm pickles in that sandwich?" I asks.

"No pickles anymore, Flannery. I can't digest them. Sit down. You want a half?"

"I can't even handle the pastrami, Dominick, pickles or no pickles."

He's looking at me over the top of his sandwich while taking a bite.

"You don't look too good, Jimmy," he says.

"Everything seems to be happening at once," I says. "The

new house, switching wards, gearing up for the council race, Mary pregnant again—"

"Your wife's going to have another baby? I didn't know that. Congratulations."

"Thanks."

He's watching me like I'm an egg and he's waiting for me to crack.

"Now this, right?" he says.

"What?"

"You ain't mentioned Mabel getting shot and killed. You ain't added that to your list of troubles and concerns."

I stare at him. Why didn't I put that on the top of my list? The murder of a friend should be number one. Is it just that I don't want to talk about what I can hardly stop thinking about?

"I hear what you're saying. What am I complaining about? Mabel Halstead saves my life and I'm complaining about all the things crowding in on me."

"Perfectly natural. It's what they call survivor remorse."

"You mean like when one person survives a plane crash and everybody else dies?"

"Same thing. Combat veterans suffer the same thing. Their best buddy gets killed and they come back to live lives they're not too sure they should still have. You got every right to live your life, Flannery. Even if you don't think you deserve it, you got a wife and a kid and another on the way, and they deserve for you to deserve to live."

It's funny, but what this tough cop says to me makes me feel a little better about myself even if I still feel very bad about what happened to Mabel.

"Thanks, Dominick."

He waves his sandwich at me.

"Don't mention it," he says.

"So, can you tell me why you called me down?"

"Well, it's been a couple of days and I'm going to ask you the same thing Captain Malloy asked you. Any chance you remembered something can give us a handle on who might've done this?"

"If anything came to mind I would've been right down here telling you about it," I says.

"Would you, Flannery? Would you? I understand you went and had a little talk with Buck Bailey yesterday."

"Discussing some of the details of him taking over the Twenty-seventh."

"That was it, was it? Just giving him a friendly hand. And that right after having a fight with him in Schaller's Pump?"

"It wasn't exactly a fight."

"He had a broken nose. That's usually the result of a blow delivered in anger."

"Or self-defense."

"I'm not going to arrest you for a barroom brawl, Flannery, though I must admit I'm a bit disappointed in you, engaging in fisticuffs like a common ruffian. It's doing the follow-up to the killing on your own that bothers me."

"I wasn't following anything up," I says.

"You and me got a long history of you going off on your own, interfering in police business," he says, ignoring my remark.

"I might have looked in places where you weren't looking, but I was never out to obstruct the police in any investigation."

"Okay. I'm not going to argue that again. I just wanted to tell you that you got no reason to keep on giving Bailey the old one-eye."

"How's that? If I meant to keep an eye on him, that is."

"Because he or Connell couldn't have been involved in the shooting because they was in the holding cell at the district station house. After you popped him and left Schaller's Pump, the boys set him up and pulled his leg until he left, getting into his car when he shouldn't. He was stopped by a cruiser and taken into custody not two blocks away. He and Connell spent the night as guests of the city."

"Can I see the booking sheet?"

"No, you can't, goddammit," Pescaro says. "What the hell's going on here? I've got to prove my veracity to you over every little goddam thing? I'm doing you a courtesy, here. I'm doing you a favor. Saving you some time and effort."

"Then Bailey wasn't booked because they found out he was the committeeman for the Twenty-seventh?"

"So what? I'm telling you he wasn't out on the street."

"Why didn't he tell me that?"

"How the hell do I know? What makes you think people got to answer to you? Give over, for Christ's sake," Pescaro says. "Have a little mercy."

"I just want to make sure that whoever might've done this thing ain't going to get off on a pass."

"No more than me. In fact, if you don't have any ideas about who might have an urgent desire to do you harm, maybe we do."

"You going to tell me?" I asks, as he finishes off the last bite of his pastrami and wipes his fingers on a napkin.

"You seeing much of Margaret Lundatos?"

"I've been stopping by. She's offered me her support and advice."

"With all the politicians and political mavens you know,

you figure a lady who spent most of her time in national politics giving parties could know something could help you?"

"She might. Her advice could be very objective. She could give me a fresh slant."

"My God, how men do bullshit themselves when a pretty piece of quim is in the picture."

I feel myself flush up and the anger rise. I'm about to take exception and then I realize that's just what he's got his eye out for.

"You went to Duluth to see her husband, didn't you?" he asks.

"He asked me to visit."

"What did he have to talk to you about?"

"What happened when he got caught with his hand in the cookie jar. Wanted to tell me no hard feelings for the threat I laid on him."

"What threat was that?"

I shake my head. "It don't signify, Pescaro. You got to trust me on this. It's got nothing to do—"

"No, you got to trust me. What threat did you lay on the Greek lion?"

"Just that I'd turn over some documentary evidence which would prove that, instead of him not knowing the building where Fay Wray was found dead, he knew all about it and was visiting her there for some rest and relaxation."

"Documentary evidence?"

"A tape I commissioned."

"Oh, Flannery, Flannery," Pescaro says. "You really do like to live out there on the edge. It's a wonder you aren't up there in the slam with your friend Lundatos."

I let it go, that little bit of sarcasm there.

"You laid a threat on him," he goes on. "He ever lay a threat on you?"

"Why would he do that?"

"He maybe doesn't like you . . . consulting . . . with his wife."

"She's obtained papers for a legal separation. She's proceeding with a divorce. He knows all about it."

"Doesn't mean he likes it. Doesn't mean he agrees with it. Doesn't mean he's ready to stand by and watch other, younger dogs come sniffing around."

"He can't put her in a box."

"Maybe he'd like to. Maybe he'd like to put her in a box. Maybe he'd like to put any special friend she might be seeing in a box, too."

"What gives you that idea?"

"He's been talking."

"Talking to who?"

Pescaro gives me a shrug for an answer, telling me what he knows is for him to know. How he knows it and why he knows it is none of my business.

"Take it as a gift from me to you," he says.

"Defeated politicians and discarded husbands like to talk," I says. "It's a matter of pride."

"You turning into a philosopher what with your elevation to high office?" Pescaro says.

"I ain't there yet."

"You be careful. You just make damn sure you live to get there. Somebody fired a gun in your direction. On a dark street. In the wee hours of the morning. From a moving car. Not your casual drive-by. Not some Latino or black gang assassin mistaking you for an enemy. Not some drunk Irishman with a grudge against you. I want you to watch out for yourself, Jimmy."

He reaches across his desk and takes my hand, holding on to it as we stand up and he comes around the desk, walking me to the door.

"Why do they call it survivor remorse?" I asks, stopping for a second before going out the door. "I don't feel guilty about anything."

"Don't kid yourself. We all feel guilty when another person dies unexpectedly and we're still alive. Don't ask me why. That's just the way it is. But if it makes you feel better saying you don't feel guilty, well, you just keep on saying it."

I drive away from police headquarters chewing on that remark.

He didn't say, That's the way it seems to be. He said, That's the way it is. All the speculation and fancy logic in the world don't apply to the world that is.

In the world that is a man can feel guilty for something he didn't do, a man can want revenge for an injury he only thinks somebody done him and things can look one way until they suddenly look another.

Don't they say that truth is stranger than fiction?

Here's a national political figure, a powerful man with a dynamite wife, who gets his hand caught in the cookie jar. Because of the temper of the times and the voters rushing to go Republican in '94, he gets put up on charges, then loses his seat in Congress, voted out by the people back home.

He don't want to give up the exercise of power so he decides, even at his age, to rebuild his career from the bottom up, going for an easy win in the city where he started out, running for alderman.

To buy a little insurance for his bet he gets a popular and

populist local politician to run with him as his party committeeman in the ward.

Meanwhile he gets caught fooling around with a call girl found dead in an apartment in a building which he claims he don't know is owned by his wife. She claims she don't know what he was up to.

For a while there he's suspect number one in the murder of the call girl.

When it proves to be her husband who done it, it still don't change the fact that his involvement is more than his running mate can stomach. Said running mate bails out on the politician.

This disgraced politician takes a plea bargain and goes away to a Club Fed for a stretch.

The ex–running mate is persuaded to seek the offices on his own. Both the jailed politician and his wife offer their blessing and support.

This is more than possible even if it's a stretch of the imagination, all these ins and outs.

Now it gets a little trickier.

The wife serves the disgraced politician with divorce papers. She becomes a friend and confidante of the almost-was running mate, which is not the kind of blessing the man in jail intended. He gets bad feelings about the man he once treated like a bosom buddy. He tells him to lay off his wife even though nothing's going on between his wife and the other guy.

Somebody takes a shot at the almost-was and he's almost dead except for a friend that takes the bullets.

Looking at it one way, it looks too complicated to be reasonable. Looking at it another, it looks simple enough to be true.

It's easy enough to contract a killing but then the customer's putting his or herself in the hands of a killer, opening themselves up to blackmail.

Just any old friend ain't going to murder somebody for you. So who do you get to do it if you can't do it yourself?

One thing's for sure, unless it was just a random shooting, whoever shot at me was tracking me or knew where I'd be that night or was just staking out the storefront in the Twenty-seventh waiting for an opportunity.

I think of all the people I can talk to about these speculations. Aunt Sada, my old man, Janet Canarias, Willy Dink or even old Dunleavy but all I'd be doing was spreading around my own fears. If whoever it was missed the first time, what's to stop them from trying to kill me some other time?

I go straight home to hug my wife, pat my dog and play with my daughter because I need a good shot of normal.

Twenty-seven

It's the middle of the night when this crazy idea sits me straight up in bed. I look at the Indiglo clock and see that it's just past one.

Mary stirs and mumbles in her sleep but don't wake up altogether, she having got used to me getting up and even going out when something hits me between the eyes like that.

I sit there playing with the notion.

There's Robert Shaftoe, this young good-looking, onetime government agent, onetime political operative, current employee of Maggie Lundatos, brought up from Washington to do what? Go through the motions of signing checks for one of her many financial organizations, a chore which could've been done by practically any accountant?

I slip out of bed, which is the wrong thing to do. You're sleeping with somebody and you want to get out of bed, just do it the way you'd do it if you was sleeping alone. Don't slip or sneak out from under the covers because that's out of the ordinary and it'll wake the other person up. Just like it wakes Mary up.

"What's the matter?" she asks.

"Nothing's the matter," I says, putting on my socks. "You go back to sleep."

"Are you just taking a pee or what?" she asks.

"I'm just going out for a little while."

She sits up then.

"What time is it?"

"One o'clock."

"What needs your attention at one o'clock in the morning?"

"It's something I got to look into, Mary, or I'll just lay here driving myself nuts all night."

"You're going out there, wandering around the city, this hour of the night?"

"There's somebody I got to see," I says.

"Maggie Lundatos?" she says, her voice flat and hard.

I sit on the bed half-dressed.

"What makes you say a thing like that?"

"I don't know. I don't know," she says. "It's the middle of the night and you tell me you're going out to see somebody and it's the first thing that popped into my head."

"I'm going to see Shaftoe."

"Why can't you call him?"

"Well, I want to see him in person. There's something I got to find out about him. I think I got a better chance of getting an answer if I'm looking at him when I ask the question."

"Why can't it wait until tomorrow?"

"I got to see him face-to-face tonight," I says. "There's nothing to fret about."

"Somebody tried to kill you and you tell me there's nothing to fret about?" she says, her voice starting to rise.

"Shh, shh, shh," I says.

"You're prowling around in the night with thieves and killers out there and you—"

"Shh, shh, shh," I says, putting my arms around her. "I ain't going anywhere that thieves and killers hang out. I'm only going to see Robert Shaftoe. I ain't going to be long."

She settles up against me and that seems to be enough to reassure her. Besides, she knows that all the protests in the world ain't going to keep me from doing something I decide to do.

I got the address of Shaftoe's flat in my address book and drive over to Argyle Street.

All the way the nursery rhyme Rourke recited is going through my mind.

> Bobby Shaftoe went to sea.
> Silver buckles on his knee.
> He'll come home and marry me.
> Pretty Bobby Shaftoe.
> Bobby Shaftoe's fine and fair.
> Combing down his auburn hair.
> He's my friend for evermore.
> Pretty Bobby Shaftoe.

Shaftoe's building ain't a security building, just a regular six-flat like the one I used to live in once upon a time. I just walk right in and climb the stairs to number four.

I ring the bell and wait. Then I ring the bell and wait again. I do that half a dozen times over five minutes and nobody comes.

Shaftoe's a young guy and there's no reason in the world why he couldn't be out on a date or hanging out in some nightclub or singles bar over on Rush. Not being home increases the chances that he could be somewhere like that but it also increases the chances that he could be somewhere else.

I drive over to Maggie's place.

I use the elevator key she gave me, waving to the night guard like I belong there, leaving him with this look on his face like he don't know if he should call up the tenant, this hour of the night, or not.

I only ring the doorbell twice with a minute in between.

She meets me at the door in a robe and barefoot.

"What's the matter, Jimmy?" she asks.

"I don't feel too good," I says, and walk right past her before she can stop me, going down the hallway on the left toward her bedroom and bathroom.

"Where are you going?" she says, her voice a little shrill, losing it a little.

"I don't want to throw up on your rug," I says, and keep walking, practically running. With her running after me in her bare feet.

I go into her bedroom and there's Shaftoe just getting into a robe, the rumpled bed behind him.

Maggie pulls up short behind me. There's no reason to try and stop me anymore. The cat's out of the bag.

"A cup of tea might be nice, Maggie," Shaftoe says.

We're in the kitchen. Maggie and Shaftoe still in their robes. I ain't even taken off my spring topcoat yet. I feel like if I started taking off my coat and jacket it could look like the beginning of an orgy or something.

Maggie turns from putting the kettle on the stove.

"Irish breakfast, Earl Grey or herb tea?" she asks.

"I'll take the herb," I says. "I might as well try and stay healthy. Eat and drink right. Watch the company I keep."

"Have you found out something about who tried to kill you?" Shaftoe says. "Is that why you came over to see Ms. Lundatos this hour of the night?"

I feel like saying something nasty about how he don't seem to need any excuse for coming over to give her a message. But I don't because all of a sudden I'm embarrassed. What am I doing acting like a jealous boyfriend or a husband what's had the horns pinned on him? I've been letting her know how I'm a happily married man with no interest in any outside action. So if she has a boyfriend that's her business and ain't got nothing to do with me. So what am I getting all hot and bothered about?

When I answer that to myself I know damned well what I'm all hot and bothered about.

"All the people I know who might think they had a reason for killing me wouldn't have the guts. I thought about every person I could think of who might work up the nerve and all I could come up with was one gazooney and his buddy who might have been dumb enough or drunk enough, but he was in no condition to've done it."

Maggie pours the hot water into the cups, drenching the tea bags she's already dropped into three white mugs. She leans back against the countertop which pushes her hips and belly forward. The top of her robe slips open. She just can't resist teasing the animals a little bit.

Shaftoe catches me looking and smiles the smile of a young man who's getting the action from an older woman and even getting paid for it with a job and wages. He's the man in control because Maggie knows that when it comes to any flirting and cheating she's the one who's got to keep an eye on him.

"So I figure it ain't an old enemy but a new one I got to think about," I says. "Maybe not even an enemy."

"What do you mean?"

"It could be an acquaintance I made just lately. It could be somebody I don't even know who was contracted to do the job by somebody else. It could be two people got reasons to do me."

"That sounds too bizarre," she says.

"Bizarre is what's making the headlines," I says. "Bizarre's getting to be commonplace."

She brings the mugs of tea over to the table. Shaftoe goes to the fridge and gets a small pitcher which he brings back to the table.

"Milk and sugar, English style?" he says.

"Not with herb tea," I says. "Sugar and lemon and not much of either."

I'm acting very classy. It's like we're stuck in a bedroom farce without the bedroom.

He goes back to the fridge and returns with a saucer filled with neat wedges of lemon.

I wonder does Maggie have somebody cut a lemon into wedges every morning. When we have use for a lemon at home, for our fish on Fridays or something like that, what's left over stays in the fridge and grows stiff until Mary throws it out.

"Bizarre," Shaftoe says, like he's reminding us to get back to the point of the conversation.

"Suppose this," I says. "Suppose this very clever, very ambitious . . . you could even say ruthless . . . lady who'd collected herself a fortune one way and another wants to get rid of a husband who ain't very useful to her anymore."

"If this speculation is about me," Maggie says in a voice as brittle as glass, "why don't you come right out with it?"

"Speaking of speculation," I says, "there was a lot of it about Leo taking bribes and tributes to the tune of a couple of million which he had stashed away for a rainy day. That's how come he could ignore the million or so in campaign contributions which, under the rules at the time, he could've put in his saddlebag when he retired.

"Suppose that wasn't a rumor. Suppose that was one of the reasons he decides to take the fall for a small one when it looks like the Republicans and the special prosecutors ain't going to stop pawing through his dirty laundry; ain't going to give up trying to nail him?

"Suppose only you, his loving and loyal wife, knows the whereabouts of that fortune and suppose you want to get your hands on it without him sharing."

"For Christ's sake, Flannery. Why are you babbling on about a couple of million dollars? I've got that to burn."

"Suppose you want to get rid of him at the same time."

"I am getting rid of him. I've filed for a legal separation and intend to file for divorce."

"I been threatened by Leo for hanging around you. On practically nothing but hearsay he's ready to believe we're rolling around in the hay. He finds out about you and Bobby here, what do you think he'll do?"

"All right," Shaftoe says, "you think you've made a case for Ms. Lundatos really and truly getting rid of Leo. Why not hire this imaginary killer to get to him up there in the Duluth Club Fed where he's raising flowers and working on his tan?"

"She can't hire a killer up there to put a shank in him because it ain't the kind of prison that accommodates such
people. But she can make it look like he killed somebody out
of jealousy over her. She could work that deal with somebody to do the actual killing of the man she wanted her husband to believe was her lover."

"Where's somebody like Ms. Lundatos going to hire a
contract killer?"

"She's already got one in her bed," I says.

"Me?" he says, like he's genuinely surprised at such a
thing.

"Why not? You got the skills. You fit the profile."

He starts to laugh then and Maggie joins right in.

When Shaftoe stops laughing, he wipes the tears from his
eyes with the back of his hand and says, "Well, you got one
thing right. We picked you to be the beard. While Leo was
looking at you he wasn't looking at me."

"You were easy," Maggie says.

Which I don't think she has to say, making me feel even
more foolish than I already feel.

"But you tell a good story though. A little complicated
but not bad. One question?"

"What?" I says.

"If you really believe that fairy tale why are you dumb
enough to come up here to make the accusation?"

"Because I didn't know you were a house pet, did I?" I
says.

His face tightens up like it was dipped in wax and his eyes
turn cold gray like they was pieces of a busted switchblade.

I get up, ready to go. I don't want a fight if I can help it.
Besides I don't think I'd have much of a chance against this
skinny guy.

He walks behind me out of the kitchen and down the hall like he's a good host showing his guest out the door. He even opens it for me.

"One thing more, Flannery."

This time I don't ask him what.

"You're really not very smart. You're so full of yourself that you fixed on the idea that somebody was out to kill *you*. Did you ever stop to think that the killer was out to get Mabel Halstead?"

Twenty-eight

I get a call from O'Meara to meet him over to Schaller's Pump.

First I go down to the police morgue to see if John Halstead's picked up Mabel's body like he said he was going to do.

Halstead ain't there to claim it. It's his daughter standing at the counter, filling out the paperwork.

We say hello and then I say, "I come down to see if I could be of any help."

"Thank you," she says. "It's not very complicated, is it? Claiming a body."

"They try to make it as easy as they can."

"How long did you know Milton?" she asks.

"Maybe ten years."

"He ever talk to you about his intentions?"

"We weren't that friendly. We just knew each other from here and there."

"But he worked for you, didn't he?"

"That was Mabel worked for me," I says.

"Sorry. I'm confused."

"So am I."

"What sort of person was Mabel?"

"Honest. Caring. Brave. Everything that your brother ever was and probably something more, something better."

The clerk checks out the forms and says, "You can take your sister's body now. I've had it placed in the mortuary car in back."

"Thank you," Mabel's sister says. "And thank you, Mr. Flannery."

I walk her around to the hearse waiting at the side entrance. We shake hands and she gets into the passenger's seat in front. Then the long black car drives away.

Schaller's Pump is pretty quiet before the lunch crowd's due to arrive, just a couple of old men sitting at one end of the bar, the day bartender in the middle and Johnny O'Meara sitting at his favorite table.

He looks up when I walk in and squints against the light pouring in behind my back through the open door.

"Nothing," I says, before the bartender can ask.

I take a chair at O'Meara's table.

"You wanted to see me, Johnny?" I asks.

"I got a call early this morning."

"Just before you called me?"

"That's right."

"Maggie Lundatos called?" I says, making it more a statement than a question.

"That's right."

"She tell you to withdraw your offer to retire and let me be appointed alderman for the rest of the term?"

"She didn't *tell* me anything," he says.

I smile like you smile at a kid trying to brag that nobody pushes him around when he's getting pushed around all over the place.

"Okay, okay," he says.

"You know I'll be running against you?"

"I figure you'd say that, now that I give you the power base from which you can build an organization in the Eleventh."

"Thanks."

"Not that it'll do you a hellofalot of good. You can't catch up on a man's put in as many years as I put into this ward."

"What choice do I have? I cut my ties to the Twenty-seventh. I don't run for alderman, I got to wonder why, and everybody else's got to wonder why, I made the switch. Whose tune was I dancing to?"

"I see what you mean."

"Whose tune are you dancing to, Johnny?"

"You got a right to think that," he says.

"Well, I sat right here while you dangled me on a hook and you were waiting for a phone call."

"I thought I could make that work, taking a little something extra to do what I didn't mind doing in the first place. Why not, right?"

"Why not?"

"It didn't go down as easy as I thought. Even that first time doing what Maggie Lundatos asked me . . . asked me . . . to do."

"I figure."

"And it ain't going down easy now, even though . . . I got to tell you . . . she sweetened the drink if I'd break my promise to you."

"Broken promises come at a price."

"No, they don't, Flannery. That's just what I'm saying. I

don't sell my promises twice. You ain't going to have to make the effort, running against me. There's going to be others from here in the Eleventh who'll reckon they can take it away from you. But, if I'm around, you'll have me in your corner and that should count for enough. We'll do it in July. The Fourth of July. I'll announce my retirement and Jim Buckey'll appoint you alderman to fill out my term of office. That suit you?"

"That suits me fine, Johnny. I want to thank you."

"Sure, sure," he says, waving my thanks off.

I start to go.

"And Jimmy?" he says. "Why don't you drop this business about who tried to kill you? It ain't going to do anybody any good keeping that pot boiling."

"I don't think anymore that whoever killed Mabel was after me, Johnny. They was after her. And, you understand, I still got to do something about that if I can."

Twenty-nine

I'm not saying it still ain't a possibility that I was the target. But after what Shaftoe says, it looks to me like it's just as good a chance that the killer got the person he was after.

So now I not only got to rack my brain trying to name everybody I ever knew who could have a grudge against me big enough to kill, but also who could have such a grudge against Milton Halstead or Mabel Halstead.

I mention this to my father while we're sitting on the porch that evening. He's been stopping by more often lately to see Kathleen when she comes home from school and hangs around long enough to chew the fat with me.

I watch the way he looks at his granddaughter, drinking her up, trying to print her little face on his memory, and it gives me a little chill. The people of his generation are dropping off one by one and only God knows how long Mike's got.

He listens to what I have to say as I tell him about my suspicions of Bailey and Connell, starting to shake his head a long time before I get to the part where I confront Bailey and, after, when Pescaro tells me Bailey was picked up two blocks from Schaller's Pump that night.

"I could've told you that Bailey never done it," Mike says. "He ain't a cold-blooded killer."

"You forgetting?"

"No, I ain't forgetting. But that was in the heat of a fight, him and Connell getting egged on by a lot of hard types who claim they never put a hand in to hurt them two poor bastards. You believe that? I'll bet you a dollar to a doughnut they wasn't the only ones put a fist or a foot into the confusion."

"Well, they was in the holding tank when the shots was fired," I says.

Then I tell him about waking up with the wacky idea of a complicated conspiracy cooked up by Maggie Lundatos to use me as a beard so she could carry on with a man young enough to be her son and the even wackier notion that he'd kill me to point the finger at Lundatos who was mouthing off about what he'd like to do to me.

"You've been busier than a cat scratching on a hot tin roof, ain't you?" Mike says, grinning like he's not altogether unhappy about the comeuppance I been handed, not once but twice.

"I could've told you that, too," he says.

"How's that?"

"Because I've had a lot more experience with women than you."

"Are you sure you want to tell me that?" I says.

"All experience don't have to be what you might call hands-on," Mike says, walking a little light here because of my memory of my mother—God rest her soul—and Charlotte, who I like very much.

"Anyways," he goes on, "you should've asked me first before going off half-cocked and invading that lady's domicile."

"I'll think twice next time," I says, handing him the win.

"So, this other possibility," he says.

He waits for me to give him some speculation but I ain't got no speculation to give him except that old grievances can surface after years and years, and new ones can flare up over something as small as a traffic dispute.

"First of all, you might even have a random-stranger killing here," Mike says. "Some kids looking to pop a citizens just for the hell of it. It might be just as easy to find somebody like that, a needle in today's haystack, than find somebody out of Milton Halstead's past and Mabel Halstead's present. The best thing you can do is let it go."

"I don't know if I can let it go."

"You got a pretty good track record, Jimmy, pulling rabbits out of hats, solving crimes even the cops couldn't or wouldn't solve, but that was then and now is now."

"What's that supposed to mean?"

Just then Kathleen's laughter comes out the open window from inside the house where she's playing with Alfie.

"That's what it means," Mike says. "You go nosing around in places you don't know nothing about and the next bullets coming your way could be meant for you. Give it up, Jimmy."

Thirty

So that's what I'm going to do. Give it up. I tell myself I ain't a cop and I ain't an avenger.

If the cops can't do it with all the resources they got, what am I supposed to do?

I'm supposed to go to work and put in my forty hours a week, because ward leader or no ward leader, I still got to work for my living. I'm supposed to take care of my wife and kids the best way I know how. I'm supposed to help the people what come to me with problems I maybe *can* do something about.

The first thing I do in the morning is contact the Halsteads to see if maybe they changed their minds about not having a funeral for Mabel.

I call the shop first because I don't really want to talk to the bereaved mother if I can help it.

A woman answers the phone, though. It's a young voice and I reckon it's Harry Cope's wife.

"Halstead Plumbing," she says.

"This is Jimmy Flannery," I says.

"Oh, yes."

"Do you know, I never got your name."

"Ellen. My name's Ellen," she says like she's not sure she should give me that information.

"I'm calling to find out if you folks changed your mind about having a service for Mabel."

"No one's changed their mind and we don't appreciate what you've done."

"I beg your pardon. What have I done?"

"Gone ahead and solicited a memorial to be held in Chicago."

"I never done nothing like that, Ellen. I ain't even heard about any such memorial."

"Have you got a fax where you're at?"

"Yes, I do," I says, and give her the number.

"I'll send a copy of what was sent to me on to you."

Before I can say anything else, she hangs up.

Three minutes later my fax machine beeps and starts kicking out a page which I read.

The top of the page shows the routing from her machine to my machine. Since it's a copy of the fax what was sent to her, I can read the routing from the originating fax to her machine.

The number looks familiar to me but I can't place it to a name because my memory for numbers, good as it is, ain't that good.

I read the long list of people the document was distributed to. Among them every city official and the whole roster of aldermen. How it got to the Halsteads I can't tell except these letters and notices are supposed to act like a chain letter, one person sending as many as they can to other people. That way, if the first person sends out ten and those ten send out three or four and those people send out even one or two, before you know it—in theory—you got the whole city covered.

The message says: "As legislation to mandate the Hate Crimes Statistics Act moves through the United States Senate, it should be noted that it does not provide for the collection of statistics concerning hate crimes against women or transgendered persons although members of these groups are often victimized.

"This letter is to inform you of the latest known hate crime against a transgendered person, which occurred recently in Chicago. Mabel Halstead was a transgendered person, having undergone gender reassignment surgery several years ago and having lived like a woman in every way since. Several nights ago, while leaving her place of employment in the office of a noted politician, she was gunned down from a moving vehicle that came out of a dark alley and sped away after the cowardly attack.

"A vigil and peaceful demonstration for Mabel Halstead will be held on Saturday beginning at 8:00 a.m. near the Picasso sculpture in Chicago's Daley Center. If you wish to attend we would welcome your presence. If you wish to have a statement read in connection with the vigil, please contact the undersigned."

It's signed Harriet Mancuso, acting for the Lobby for GenderPAC.

I go into my electronic Rolodex looking for the number of the fax that sent the message, telling myself I got to learn how to set up an address book on a computer so I can search the files by home number, work number, address, occupation, name and so forth, instead of fingering through a whole collection.

The way I work it is, new numbers, like a month old, go into a special little section before I move them up to the permanent location. But I don't find a thing.

I type out a page that says, "I would be interested to know who belongs to your fax machine," and sign it and send it, hoping I'll get an answer back sometime soon.

My fax starts to beep and buzz within five minutes and out comes a page what says, "You're right. I sometimes think I'm owned by my VCR, fax, computer, and every LED provided on nearly every appliance one buys nowadays. This is Lloyd Moraine and if you'll fax me the telephone number where you are at the moment, I will call you within the hour. Or you can call me at home."

He's typed out the number there on the page he sends me, so I reach for the phone and dial him up.

The phone's picked up on the other end before it can ring more than twice.

"Flannery?" Moraine's dry, Yankee voice says.

"Yes, sir, it's me."

"You got the notice of the memorial Mary sent you? I meant to follow it up with a personal telephone call but the day got away from me."

"I didn't get it direct," I says. "How is your wife?"

"Better. A little better. But it's slow going. You say you didn't get your own copy from GenderPAC? How did you get it?"

"Ellen Cope, Mabel's sister over to Deerfield, sent me a copy."

"Oh, good."

"No, not good. She told me that her family wanted a quiet end to everything. No memorials or services."

"Well, we don't always get what we want. Sometimes there are larger issues."

"Which is the way I feel about the banning of books."

I hear another voice, Mary's voice, coming through the receiver and I hear Lloyd replying to her, not bothering to cover the mouthpiece but turning his head away.

When he comes back on clear, he says, "Mary wants to talk to you herself."

"Hello, Jimmy," Mary's voice, a little weaker than last I heard her speak, but still driven by this terrific energy she's got, says like we been friends for a hundred years.

"How are you feeling?"

"I'm feeling my age, sweetheart," she says. "I hope no one will be offended by the memorial my organization's going to hold this Saturday."

"Your organization?"

"Well, I've been president, vice president and treasurer at one time or another. Right now I'm what they call an honored member. We think it's important to draw public attention to hate crimes. Crimes against women and children and anyone else who's victimized by the hatemongers. Like you were against those men you put away. The men who beat those two homosexuals to death."

"You remember that case?"

"When it happened, I was president of another humanist organization that was the parent of the organization that's holding the memorial," she says. "I used to be very busy with organizations."

"And will be again."

"Don't get conventional on me, Jimmy. I wish you'd do me a favor."

"Anything I can do."

"Talk to the Halstead family for me. Try to make them understand why we think this service necessary. Make it clear to them it's not being done to embarrass or shame them."

"I'll do it first thing."

"Do it in person, if you can."

"First chance I get."

"Are you going to be at the memorial service?" she asks.

"Yes, I certainly will."

"You'll have your chance to speak to the Halsteads then," she says. "If I know human nature, they'll be there."

Her voice is getting soft and thready. I know she's tiring herself.

"Well, good-bye, Jimmy. See you later."

"See you later, alligator," I says.

"That's what we used to say years ago," she says, and laughs. "Here's Lloyd."

Lloyd gets back on the phone.

"Mary probably won't be there, but I will. We'll talk some more about this book banning after the ceremony. Saturday, then. See you at the dog."

Thirty-one

The dog sitting in Daley Center, as every citizen and visitor to Chicago knows, is the big red steel cutout given to the city by Picasso back in 1967. Not everybody calls it a dog, of course. This 163-ton pile of Cor-Ten steel has been called a dodo bird, the head of a woman with flowing hair, a baboon and a lawyer with a briefcase.

It caused a lot of controversy when it was first put up and there was many who wanted Picasso to take it back. But now it's an object of some affection, a landmark of the town where people meet.

I'm there at ten minutes to eight on Saturday morning. It's a beautiful day, the first real day of spring weather. The clouds in the blue sky are small and look like a flock of sheep drifting above the city.

Even that early, there's plenty of people around, youngsters kicking them little bags of beans around. Some, young and old, on Rollerblades. A few business types in suits and ties determined to make their fortunes by putting in a little or a lot of overtime.

The people from the Lobby for GenderPAC have a very small banner set up between two poles. Nothing gaudy or bold. Just something to draw people's attention so they know the ceremony is going to take place over there by the curb.

Off in a cluster all by themselves I see John Halstead and a younger man who looks just like him, both of them dressed in suits and ties. An older woman with a sweater thrown over her dress is standing next to John. Harry Cope is with his wife, Ellen, but neither one is dressed much different than I see them dressed in the plumbing shop.

They're standing on the very edge of the sidewalk, closest to the street. I walk over to greet them.

John Halstead doesn't stick out his hand to me.

"Hello, Mr. Flannery," he says. "This is my son, Jack, flew in last night."

Jack puts out his hand and we shake.

"You spoke to my wife on the telephone," John Halstead goes on.

"Yes, ma'am," I says, and she shakes my hand, too. She's wearing gloves like she was dressed for church.

Then I say hello to Harry and Ellen and shake their hands.

I look at John again and he finally puts his hand out too.

"I was asked to deliver a message to you from an honored member of this organization what's doing this memorial. Her name's Mary Moraine and she's been fighting things like prejudice and bigots all her life. She wanted you to know this ain't being done to give away your secrets or your family's private business . . ."

John Halstead holds up his hand with the palm toward

me, so I run down and don't complete what I was going to
say.

"Thank her for us," he says. "We can see the way our
child died should be noticed and remembered."

My back's to the street and the celebrants.

I start turning around when I hear the beginning of a
hymn. At that same moment my body starts to crouch and
duck—just like I read about how veterans who been through
shelling in combat'll do when they first come home—because
I hear the sound of an engine that's banging out of synch in a
distinctive way. The exact same sound that I heard twice before. Once in the parking lot outside Bochos school and once
when the headlights washed over me in the doorway of the office just before I heard the shots and Mabel pushed me
through the glass. It's the one little thing every cop what ques-
tioned me was hoping they could jar loose, that detail you forgot and don't even know you forgot until a similar event brings
it all back in a rush.

Jack Halstead must think I'm stumbling and falling because he reaches out a hand to save me and he's half holding
me up, me looking up at the driver of the car, when Asbach
steps out into the street and looks directly at me.

Right that minute I know he killed Mabel and he knows I
know it.

Thirty-two

I'm not going to say much about the memorial service, the speeches and the nondenominational hymn singing.

It was all right, the way such things are, but, for some reason I can't explain, that kind of thing always seems a little off to me. Maybe because I can't shake the feeling that this or that organization is exploiting somebody what's been victimized. Like a lot of these trials where the dead person gets trashed by the lawyers trying to save the killer or claim mitigation for the crime. They act like it's a good thing to do or, at least, it's something that they got to do for the greater good.

The Halsteads seemed comforted by it, so maybe it was a good thing after all.

I don't know if Asbach was comforted by it though.

I watched him throughout the whole thing which lasted maybe fifteen minutes.

After locking eyes with me when he stepped out of the car, he kept his eyes on the speakers and the singers, and never looked at me again until it was over.

By that time a cop has wandered over to tell Asbach he can't park there. Asbach nods and says something to the cop, then waves me over.

I say a quick good-bye to the Halsteads and go over to get into Asbach's car. He's already behind the wheel.

He don't say a word to me or me a word to him as he drives away from Daley Center down Washington Boulevard until we come to this little café on North La Salle.

The morning's warmed up pretty good—it's almost like early summer—and the café owner's taken the opportunity to move some tables and chairs out on the sidewalk for a little touch of Paris.

Asbach sits down at one of the tables. A waiter pops out to take our orders. We both ask for coffee though I don't drink much coffee lately, it having a tendency to keep me awake at night.

"I suppose you'd say I got what I deserved," he says.

"Not yet, you ain't," I says.

"I mean a man who's fought for certain moral principles falling in love with a sexual freak."

"When it comes to moral principles, you ain't learned much," I says.

He stares at me with this vague expression as though he's lost in a dream, taking no offense from what I just says to him.

"You don't know a thing, Flannery," he says, like it's a sad thing to have to say.

"I know that you been making your living sticking your nose into things where it don't belong," I says. "I know you think you know better than anybody else what God wants."

"The anti-abortion movement I was involved in was like my ministry. You wouldn't think it strange that a priest or reverend made a living preaching in his church and tending to his flock."

"This book banning you're doing from the school council. Is that just a little pro bono meddling?"

"That's personal. I have my daughter to consider. There's no payment for serving on the council."

"So just what are you doing to pay the rent, Asbach?" I asks.

He waves that off like it's of no consequence. I agree, it ain't of any consequence.

"What about Mabel?" I asks. "I know you got fooled by Mabel Halstead and you shot and killed her."

"I met her at your coronation," he says, giving it a little of the twisty, sarcastic lip.

"I saw you eyeing her up."

"I drove her home that night."

"I figured."

"I saw her very often after that. I found her the most attractive woman I'd met in a long time."

I want him to get to the reason for him killing her but I know if I push too hard he'll clam up and tell me to go to hell. So I just sit, letting him tell it his own way and in his own time. It's like he's talking to hisself, reliving what he calls his courtship of Mabel Halstead.

"Things can develop between two people, a man and a woman, very rapidly in today's world. Even children are having sexual intercourse after one or two meetings. I didn't want to have it that way. I wanted a courtship and I was pleased to find out that . . . she . . ." He stumbles over the word like it got stuck in his throat for a second. "That she wanted the same thing. We were going to explore one another's minds before we went on to explore our bodies."

He stops talking and just stares off. It lasts so long I'm about to say something to get him going again.

But then he goes on.

"There's a saying I heard in Sweden once long ago, when I was a very young man. 'First comes the love of the body and then comes the love of the heart.' I don't believe that's the moral thing to do or believe."

I don't say anything because he's not really talking to me but to hisself and that's just the way I want it.

"John Donne wrote differently. He said, 'Love in the heart doth grow but the body is the book.' "

He shakes his head as though he's rejecting that, too. Or maybe it's just showing his confusion. He's deep into his thoughts and feelings. I ain't even there for him anymore. His voice is dreamy and husky, remembering.

"Well, sooner or later we seek physical intimacy, don't we? And that night I thought it time to consummate the love we clearly felt for one another. We had touched and explored before, satisfied each other in several ways, but we'd never lain together and really shared ourselves. Then, suddenly, as we lay there naked, she demurred. She tried to stop me having her. I thought it was some odd way of teasing me, driving me to greater arousal, perhaps. She ordered me to stop but I persisted, feeling that she was big enough and strong enough to get away from me if she really wanted to. Afterward . . ."

His face twists and he stops talking, all choked up with rage, not sexual passion, now.

"It was then she . . . he . . . it told me what it was. I was sick. I felt such a revulsion. I threw up immediately, fouling the bed as I'd been fouled. Halstead got dressed and fled and left me there alone with my terrible revulsion and shame."

The sounds of the city return like a switch was thrown, I been listening so hard to what he says.

He turns his eyes to me again and looks at me as though expecting me to agree with him about what a terrible thing was done to him.

"Then you decided to hunt her down," I says.

"If not at home, I knew Halstead would look for a friend with whom . . ."

When he hesitates again, not willing to say the word, I fill it in for him. "She," I says. "She."

He shrugs as though it ain't an issue big enough to argue about.

"I knew she'd seek you or Janet Canarias out. I don't think she had any other friends."

"Except she thought she had you," I says.

"Anyway, I knew where to look," he says.

"Did it relieve you of your hate?"

"I didn't hate her," he says, like he's surprised I should even think such a thing.

"What are you going to do about it now?" I asks.

"Do what? Turn myself in? Stand trial? Ask to pay the price for killing her? I don't intend to do anything except live with what I've done and try to be a better person."

"Now it's me who's going to throw up," I says.

He stands up and tosses two bucks down on the table for the coffee. The wise-guy arrogance comes back into his face and posture.

"And what are you going to do, Flannery? How are you ever going to prove what I just told you? How are you even going to prove I ever told you?"

I sit there drinking the cold remains of the coffee and thinking about what he just said, the challenge he just tossed in my face. I reach into my pocket and take out the miniature tape recorder I carry around with me ever since my plate gets so full I can't hardly remember one appointment to the next.

My name's Jimmy Flannery and I'm marching toward the millennium, trying the best I can to deal with VCRs and microwaves and satellite dishes and computers and the Internet and . . .

One thing I know ain't going to change all that much. Human nature. I'm doing the best I can trying to understand that.